SMALL ACCIDENTS

SMALL ACCIDENTS

BY

ANDREW GRAY

RAINCOAST BOOKS

Vancouver

Raincoast Books acknowledges the ongoing support of The Canada Council; the British Columbia Ministry of Small Business, Tourism and Culture through the BC Arts Council; and the Government of Canada through the Book Publishing Industry Development Program (BPIDP).

First published in 2001 by

Raincoast Books
9050 Shaughnessy Street
Vancouver, B.C.
V6P 6E5
(604) 323-7100

www.raincoast.com

Edited by Joy Gugeler
Cover photo copyright 2001 ©PhotoDisc, Inc.
Cover design by Val Speidel

1 2 3 4 5 6 7 8 9 10

CANADIAN CATALOGUING IN PUBLICATION DATA
National Library of Canada Cataloguing in Publication Data

Gray, Andrew (Andrew Neil), 1968-
   Small accidents

   ISBN 1-55192-508-7

   I. Title.
PS8563.R3953S62 2001   C813'.6   C2001-910846-X
PR9199.4.G72S62 2001

At Raincoast Books we are committed to protecting the environment and to the responsible use of natural resources. We are acting on this commitment by working with suppliers and printers to phase out our use of paper produced from ancient forests — this book is one step towards that goal. It is printed on 100% ancient-forest-free paper (100% post-consumer recycled), processed chlorine- and acid-free, and supplied by New Leaf Paper; it is printed with vegetable-based inks by Friesens. For further information, visit our website at www.raincoast.com. We are working with Markets Initiative (www.oldgrowthfree.com) on this project.

Printed and bound in Canada

For Jennifer

CONTENTS

OUTSIDE

For more than a week now my wife has been sleeping in a tent in the backyard. The tent is small; a two-man pup that can sleep only one in any comfort. She couldn't find the propane stove we bought at the same time, so I've been taking her dinner out to her.

I've cooked an omelette for the second night in a row. I'm home late from work and I can't think of anything else. I take it to her on a tray with a glass of milk and a couple of fresh batteries for her flashlight.

"You know how much cholesterol this has?" she says from inside the tent. "You'll turn my arteries to concrete. You're not running out of groceries, are you?"

"Sorry," I say. "I haven't cooked since university."

"I remember." She reaches up and takes the tray from me. "It's okay. Thanks." I look past her into the tent and see her sleeping bag, half unzipped, some candy wrappers, a small mound of books. One of the books is open on her pillow. She looks at me for a moment and I can see her eyes are still bruised and dark. She reaches for the zipper.

"You're welcome," I say, but all I hear is the clink of her fork on the plate.

I sit in the kitchen for a while eating my own omelette and reading the paper. Out in the yard the tent glows like a blue lantern. Every so often I see her outlined against the nylon as she changes position.

My wrist has been itchy the last couple of days and I've found myself absently poking my knife under the cast. When I was thirteen I broke the same wrist falling off my bike. I'd ignored the doctor and got it wet in the shower, in the swimming pool. It started to rot inside and eventually got so bad I had to leave class and go to the hospital for a new one; kids were getting sick from the smell.

The cast I wear now is fibreglass; I can wear it in the shower.

The red light on the answering machine pulses silently, signalling a host of unanswered calls: insurance, the doctor about my wrist or Sarah's leg, the secretary from the community college where she teaches part-time. I haven't answered the phone for four days. I haven't written down any messages either.

I look into the yard and see Sarah has put her tray outside the tent door. I go out to pick it up and sit down on the slightly damp lawn. I can hear her steadily turning pages. She is humming softly.

"I don't have anything to say," she says, startling me. I

don't respond, wondering if she is talking to herself.

"Fraser," she says. "I can hear you sitting out there — you wheeze like a smoker, you know."

"I've started up again," I say.

"It's got nothing to do with me," she says. "They're your lungs."

"Do you need anything else?"

"Go back inside," she says. "Go to bed."

I open one of the single malts we keep in the bar to impress guests and sit in the kitchen drinking slowly while the dishwasher sloshes behind me. The last time we used the tent was three or four years ago, canoeing in Algonquin. Four days of clean air and campfires. We zipped the sleeping bags together and made love every night. I imagine pine needles scattered under her pillow, the smell of the forest still filling the tent.

We always planned to go again, to make it a yearly trip, but I haven't been able to get the time off or find the energy.

The next morning I see Dr. Wells again, my head still throbbing from the whisky. She looks at my wrist, the cut on my forehead, my ribs.

"Careful," I say, as she taps my chest.

"You're healing well," she says. "You know, if it weren't for that airbag, you probably wouldn't have any broken ribs at all."

It had been like hitting a wall. I'd been half-deafened by the sound of it.

"Where's Sarah?" she asks. "I wanted to see both of you."

"She couldn't make it," I tell her. "But she's doing well."

The doctor shakes her head. "Tell her to come in Monday, then — no more excuses."

I drive the rental car to the plant, struggling a little with the stick shift. Sarah has a Honda Civic at home, but I've left it for her in case she needs to go out. She hasn't touched it. Damp towels and vanishing food are the only signs she's actually leaving the tent.

Things have been bad at work all week, so I've been putting in a lot of overtime. We had a six-hour shutdown in Liquids Packing and are still trying to catch up. Little crises keep slowing us down: broken conveyors, faulty sensors, plastic chips appearing in the soap.

Beekman calls me into his office as I pass reception.

"Fraser," he says. "We're going with that extra shift in Liquids on Saturday to make up for the shutdown."

I'd suggested it earlier in the week. "Makes sense," I say. "I'll come in to keep an eye on things."

"No, there's no need. I'll get one of the area managers to do it."

"It's no problem," I say. "I don't mind."

Beekman clears his throat. He looks a little uncomfortable. "Look," he says. "There's no reason for you to be in here on Saturday." He smiles a little. "I'm playing golf myself. Why don't you leave early today? You've only had one day off since your accident. I don't want you to burn out."

"I'm fine," I say. "Really, I'd like to do it."

"Go home, Fraser. Okay?" He sits down in his chair, taps a couple of keys on his computer. "I'm serious." He turns to his screen, dismissing me.

I review some files, answer the morning's e-mail and phone messages, type up a memo for the area managers. I'm staring distractedly at my computer screen when Laura, the receptionist, pokes her head through the door. "Oh, sorry," she says. "Beekman told me you'd left. I was just shutting off your lights."

"I'm — " I look at the files on my desk, the unfinished list in my daytimer and suddenly feel very tired. "I'm just packing up," I say.

The traffic is heavy already, people heading off to their cottages for the weekend. When I get home I realize I've been on autopilot the whole way. As I step out of the car, the humid air wraps itself around me and I start to sweat. I can feel the solid weight of fatigue in me — something I've had so long it almost feels comforting.

I take off my tie, unbutton my shirt and pour a glass of orange juice. I start rummaging around in the cupboards for an ashtray; then I realize I've been hearing water running since I came in. I walk up the stairs to the bathroom and see Sarah's shoes in front of the door. I turn and walk back downstairs and outside to the tent. I unzip the flaps and crawl inside. It is hot in the tent, everything tinged blue. It smells vaguely of her, slightly musky and damp. I lie on the sleeping bag for a minute and imagine her at night with her flashlight and her books, her head full of thoughts.

I pick up a book called *Cancer Ward*, another called *Couples*. I've never been able to make it past the first chapter of any of her books. They all seem so formal, as if the author is giving a speech. I get enough of that at work.

In the house the shower is still running. I stand in the kitchen like a burglar, wondering if I should leave. It doesn't feel like our house anymore. I walk upstairs and see Sarah standing in the bathroom doorway, naked, towelling her hair. Water trickles down her arms and legs and drips onto the carpet. Her skin is flushed from the heat. She has bruises on her arms and black tangled stitches, like the seam on a pair of stockings, run up her leg. I see the slight curve of her stomach, the dark tuft below and imagine the smell of her wet hair, her scrubbed skin.

She moves the towel down her body and then looks up.

"You haven't been fired, have you?" she asks.

"What?"

"You're home so early." She pats the towel gently around her stitches, wincing slightly.

"No," I say. "Beekman told me to take the rest of the afternoon off."

"So it wasn't your decision to come home?"

"Have you come back inside now?"

"You're changing the subject. You would have stayed

at work, wouldn't you?" She towels her hair.

"At least when I'm here, I'm here," I say. "Some people wouldn't bring you your dinner out there, you know."

She doesn't answer, but walks over to her bureau and pulls on underwear, fastens her bra. I stand there as she dresses and walks out of the room.

I spend the rest of the afternoon on the deck in my shorts, shirtless, reading the paper and drinking the last of the Heineken from the fridge. The bottles are cold and solid in my hand. The paper is full of words I have to read over and over to understand. Sarah is in her tent. I hear the sound of traffic from two blocks over, a sprinkler whirring nearby.

We've had the house almost three years now. We'd talked of children, of the market being right, low interest rates. Sarah's parents loaned us some money. But the house was really an attempt to find permanence. I think we both knew it. We've got a mortgage, two cars, a lawn. We haven't talked about kids for a while, but I cut the lawn every week, wash the cars a couple of Sundays a month, shovel the driveway when it snows. I cook now, vacuum the rug. Except for the tent, we look like everyone else on the street. The tent is a new development.

Sarah and I were at a party. I was supposed to drive home, but a friend of mine from work was there and I ended up talking shop most of the night and drinking more than

I'd planned. Sarah wasn't too impressed, so I gave her the keys. She drove at fifteen or twenty over legal, her face glowing in the green light from the dash, the flare of headlights passing. It was raining. Something soft played on the radio. My eyes were closed when I felt the car hit the shoulder and start to skid. I called out her name. The car spun around, flipped over and then we skidded on the roof, gravel pouring in through the broken windows. The car hit something and the airbags went off like bombs, kicking me in the chest.

It is dusk by the time I finish all the beer. Sarah's flashlight has clicked on. I pull out a pack of Marlboros and light one up, sucking the harsh smoke deep into my lungs. I feel confident, maybe even reckless.

I go down onto the lawn and crouch in front of the tent, the cigarette a spark in my left hand. "Come back to the house," I say.

Silence.

I tug on the zipper. She frowns at me. "Please don't."

"No. This is crazy; we can't keep on like this. It was an accident, for Christ's sake." I feel a rush of sympathy for her, for her bruised eyes and scars. "I'm not blaming you, you know. It could have happened to me just as easily. Anyway, I was the one who had too much to drink."

"It's not just the accident ...," she says. "But it was my fault."

"What?"

"It wasn't the rain," she says. "It was me. We just started heading toward the shoulder and I didn't do anything to stop it."

I had blacked out for a minute. There were faint voices outside the car. I hung from the seatbelt, my pulse pounding in my head. When I released the belt I hit the roof of the car and felt a flash of pain. My mind was muddled; I was in shock. I looked at Sarah hanging in the driver's seat. Her eyes were open. For a terrible moment I thought she was dead, but then she blinked and I felt a wave of relief. I wanted to say something then, but there was only the tick of cooling metal and the calls of the strangers who had pulled over and were coming to help. We stared at each other.

"What about the tent?" I finally ask. "You can't stay out here forever. It won't change anything."

"Will staying *inside* change anything?" she asks. "Anyway, I don't think I'm the one who needs to change."

I look back at the house. It sits squat and dark in the dim light. "Whatever." I get up, needing to move.

I turn on the TV, flip light switches, climb the stairs and go into our bedroom. I sit in front of her bookshelf for a while, reading unfamiliar names. I try to imagine how it must look to her at night, seeing me sitting at the window. During the day she showers and eats and walks around in the quiet house. She lies on the couch or in the tent and reads her books. What does she find in them?

On our camping trip we lay on the smooth granite beside the lake, ignoring the insects, the sky pulsing with stars. She invented names for them, making up stories about haunted lovers and boys who defied gods. I laughed and told her she was a liar. "Why not?" she asked. "All the best stories are lies."

The tent is dark when I walk back outside, the house bright behind me. I take off my shoes, open the zipper slowly and crawl inside. Sarah's eyes are open. I lie down beside her and she turns to face me. "Maybe you should read me something," I say softly.

She puts her hand lightly on my chest and leaves it there. "Shh," she says, "shh."

SMALL ACCIDENTS

The night after he was unfaithful to her, Simon lay in bed with his wife, listening to the sounds of his in-law's house and waiting for sleep to claim him. The clock in the hall ticked steadily and one of the dogs padded past the door, its nails clicking on the floor. Beside him, Maria gave a small sigh and turned over. He wanted to wake her and say, "Don't you see? This is the type of man I am," but he couldn't imagine what might happen next. Instead, he got up and went into the washroom, opened the window and had one of his rare cigarettes. Nocturnal insects fluttered in and banged against the bare bulb, fell dazed to the floor.

The next morning he walked along the river with Maria's parents. They passed the small grove of trees where he and Pam had been the day before and he looked away, focusing on the mud and stones of the shore. There had been a storm the previous morning and branches littered the water's edge. The river was dark as coffee.

The dead deer looked like a bundle of old clothing. The dogs noticed it first and raced ahead, scaring up a cloud of crows. Simon followed behind Maria's parents as they walked toward it, poking at the mud with a stick. They all stopped beside the body. The crows hopped cautiously down the riverbank, waiting for them to leave. Simon nudged the head with his sneaker. The animal's fur was swirled and tufted, licked clean by the river. There was no obvious cause of death.

"They don't just fall in, do they?" Simon sniffed cautiously, wondering if it had started to rot.

Maria's mother walked carefully around it in her rubber boots, making small squelching sounds in the mud. "I doubt it. Might be a bullet in this one somewhere we can't see."

"Probably hit by a car." Maria's father held an insulated coffee mug with the word CHIEF printed on the side. He took a sip. "It stumbled off to die and got washed downstream."

He waved his walking stick at the dogs. "Alex, come off it." The big German shepherd was nosing around the side of the deer, sniffing intently. They passed the corpse and he whistled for the dogs to catch up. As they headed along the riverbank past the dock and up to the house, Simon looked back at the body, at the dark, sluggish river. The air was musty and ripe, with a trace of salt and the fermenting tang of mud.

At the house, Simon sat on the wide back veranda looking down at the river's slow procession toward the ocean. He imagined for a moment it was the land that was moving, turning slowly through the water, heading upstream. He balanced a bowl of cereal on his knees, held a mug of tea.

He hadn't planned on sleeping with Pam; it wasn't one of the things he had thought about as he put on his shorts the morning before. How could he have known that as his wife lay by her parent's pool drinking mint juleps later that day, his shorts and shirt would be in a small heap beside him and he would be caressing the bare breasts of her younger sister? It hadn't crossed his mind at all.

Maria wouldn't have done anything so impulsive. She wasn't the sort of person who just stumbled into things. She always looked a choice up and down before making it. He remembered the day he'd asked her to marry him. She'd given him the same sort of look she might have given a car salesman when it came time to get down to the hard bargaining. A sharp, intelligent appraisal. "Yes," she said finally, "I will."

In that moment before she answered, he had absolutely no idea what she was thinking.

Not that he blamed her for the current situation; it was obvious that he hadn't turned out to be quite the person she'd wanted, that his stability, his dependability, could be seen as a reluctance to get fully involved in things, a reliance on the safety of routine. He remembered saying to her one night, "I guess the honeymoon's over," terribly aware how much it sounded like a line from a bad movie. She had been complaining things weren't the same between them anymore. He'd felt bad, but he'd thought she should know that a marriage had its phases, like the moon. They just happened to be in one of the dimmer ones.

After breakfast, he and Maria drove into town. He felt as tongue-tied and nervous as he had when they were first dating. He waited in stores while she tried on dresses and shoes. He bought her an ice cream cone. They walked along the streets like other couples. *Maybe we* are *like other couples*, he thought.

They bumped into Pam on the main street, coming out of the store where she worked. "Hey, there," she said. "Miss me?"

"You have no idea," Maria said.

"There's a dead deer on the shore near the dock," Simon said. He found himself blushing as he said it and turned away, clearing his throat.

"I'm bringing the boys over again today. You'll have to show me." Pam turned to Maria. "Did you have a look?"

"Not a chance," she said. "You know me." She had been the type of child who had always brought home injured birds and squirrels. Once, when she and Simon passed the body of a dog on the side of the road, she had made him pick it up and take it to the humane society. She couldn't bear the thought of its owner not knowing what had happened, thinking it had run away. It had taken weeks before the smell faded from the back seat.

"It's just a deer," Simon said. "Things die all the time."

Maria frowned at him and then gave Pam a small, unconvincing smile. "We'd better get going," she said.

Farther down the street, Simon said, "She's not *that* bad, you know."

Maria snorted. "You know she's made a mess of her life. She drinks too much and Harv left her because she fooled around too much."

"How much is too much?"

She glanced at him. "I don't know," she said. "Obviously she found out."

"Most people would say once is too much."

"That marriage was doomed from the start," she said. "She was drunk on her wedding day, remember? *Before* the ceremony. Adultery was the nail in the coffin."

"You mean the straw that broke the camel's back."

"Whatever," she said. "I'll just be a second." She ducked into the washroom of a restaurant called "Moby's," stepping cautiously past the faded white fibreglass whale that loomed in the entranceway. Simon sat on the edge of the sidewalk and watched a group of young boys on skateboards hurl themselves at a sloping concrete barrier across the street.

A few weeks before, he'd come home from work on his lunch break, looking for some files he'd left in the living room. When he got to the house there was an unfamiliar car in the driveway, a dark BMW. He'd felt his heart lurch. He parked on the street and walked around back. He wasn't sure what he'd expected — something torrid perhaps, skin gleaming through a window, a trail of clothing. Instead he'd seen Maria in the garden with George, the dentist from the practice where she worked. They were eating lunch.

He relaxed, feeling slightly foolish. As he tried to think of an innocuous greeting to announce himself, George leaned forward and casually dabbed his napkin at the corner of Maria's mouth. It was such an intimate gesture that Simon's knees buckled and he had to put his hand on the wall to steady himself.

He sat in his car for a while, appraising the mundanity of it all: the unexpected return home, the car in the driveway. It was such a cliché. According to his plan for them they should have been putting their first child into daycare, Maria should have been wearing flowery sundresses. They were supposed to be vacationing on a lake somewhere, making home movies.

When she came out of the restaurant he was still watching the skateboarders. She walked up behind him and kissed him on the back of his neck. "Hey," she said.

He twitched suddenly, startled. "Hi," he said, without turning around.

She sat beside him. "Deep in thought?"

"Maybe I should take up skateboarding," he said. "Would that make me more interesting?"

She laughed. "Sure," she said. "I'll tell the hospital to expect you."

After lunch they sunbathed by the pool. Maria lay beside him, reading. She sipped from her can of beer, dipped a piece of pita in some hummus. Simon couldn't concentrate on his book, a mystery. All the characters were mixed up in his mind and he kept forgetting which one was the victim, who might be guilty. Eventually he gave up and drifted, drowsy with the heat.

The slam of a car door woke him. Pam's car was beside the rental they had picked up at the airport and she was herding her son Trevor and two other small boys toward them. "Hi," she yelled as she saw Maria and Simon. She opened the gate and the boys ran to the pool, stripping down to their trunks and leaping in. Pam waved and sat on one of the loungers, taking off her shorts to reveal the rest of her one-piece swimsuit. "Mom and Dad not around?" she asked.

Maria looked up from her book. "They're off to the city for the day. They'll be back at nine or ten tonight."

"Oh," Pam said. "Maybe we won't stay for dinner, then." She took a bottle of tanning oil from her bag, coated her face and arms and settled back into the chair with a magazine.

The boys yelled and fought. They splashed each other, leaped from the diving board, called to the adults to watch. Pam looked up every so often to applaud a particularly messy dive. Maria read and took careful bites of her pita, eyes invisible behind her sunglasses. Simon tried not to look at Pam.

After he and Maria had been married a year, Simon had brought up the subject of children. "It's about time," he had said.

Maria had shaken her head. "Not yet. Not nearly. We're young. We've got some money. You don't want to be dull, do you?"

"I suppose not," he'd said reluctantly, but secretly he craved dullness. Sometimes he wished he and Maria were retired already, emotional turbulence long behind them, their children grown and away. He would have a garden to work in, they would take a yearly trip south in the winter, go on long walks. He found he envied Maria's parents for the quiet calm of their relationship, especially in contrast to his own mother and father, who had divorced when he was sixteen. Sometimes he felt he got along better with her parents than with Maria. The three of them certainly had more in common.

After a couple of minutes Simon got up and lumbered into the pool. The boys climbed his back, grabbed his arms and legs and he slowly slid underwater with them, a toppling giant. When they surfaced, spluttering and laughing, Pam slid into the water beside him.

"Now there are two monsters in here," she said. She bobbed beside Simon in the shallow end, seal-like in her dark suit. She touched his leg with her foot. "You'll have to show me the deer soon."

He felt nervous. "It's not that big a deal," he said. "It might have washed away by now, anyway."

She laughed. "Come on," she said. "How often do I get a chance to see a good corpse?" She ducked under the surface. He felt her hair brush past him as she kicked toward the deep end, moving like a shadow through the water. When she climbed out, she towelled off and went up to the house for more beer and some drinks for the kids. Simon watched her for a moment as she walked across the grass. Her dark hair swung wet against her tanned shoulders, muscles moved in her back and legs.

He had been on the dock the day before, drowsy in the heat, the sound of the kids in the pool nearby floating through the air with the hum of insects in the long grass. The wood creaked and small waves slapped against the side of the boat tied there. Branches floated past, minnows hung in the shadows. There was a rustle behind him and he turned to see Pam walking down the low hill that sloped from the yard to the water. "Hey," she said as she came onto the dock and sat beside him. "You've got company." She dipped her feet in the water.

"Maria sleeping?" he asked.

"She's still reading, keeping an eye on the boys." Pam lifted her feet in and out of the river, watching the water drip from them, making patterns. "I thought I'd come and catch up with you." She splashed him and he looked at the drops on his legs, the tiny lenses gleaming with light.

He watched her feet swinging back and forth for a

moment and then stood up. "Want to take a stroll?"

They walked barefoot through the sand and mud toward the trees, stepping over the branches washed up by the storm. Through the trees they came to a small, grassy clearing. "I used to hide here when I was a kid," she said.

"From Maria?"

She smiled. "Sure, sometimes. The world in general." She sat down and patted the grass beside her.

He sat carefully. "You still come here?"

She looked at him. "It's nice to escape. I need to get away sometimes, you know."

"I know," he said. "I know."

She had flirted with him from the first day they'd met, when Maria brought him to meet her parents. He'd indulged her, enjoying the banter, something he'd never quite been able to manage before. He'd always sounded either lecherous or false.

"You're a sweet guy," she said.

"I know that, too," he said, dejectedly. He had always been the confidante, the steady third wheel. He took girls out for lunch when they had been dumped, comforted them over chicken salad sandwiches. He cooked dinners, bought flowers, sent thank-you notes. He couldn't imagine how he would confront Maria about her affair. Every time he tried to run through the scene in his head it felt false. Another man would do it better, would know exactly what to say.

He looked over and saw Pam was studying him. He

leaned over and kissed her quickly, his heart beating faster with the audacity of it. She looked back at him, surprised, then he saw a familiar look flit across her face. She was figuring things out, appraising. She kissed him back.

He moved his fingers over her, heard her breath whistle through her nostrils, felt his heart thudding in his chest. When they lay down, her hair tangled in the grass. He watched the progress of an ant as it navigated around their bodies. The skin under her bathing suit was pale and smooth. His dark hands moved over it as if they belonged to someone else.

She cried out, the high sound rising through the air like the call of an animal. The wind carried the sound of the children in the pool. Above, poplar leaves fluttered like flags in a parade, like applause, the clapping of thousands of tiny hands.

When it was over, he lay beside her, breathing heavily. He felt the lust evaporate into emptiness. She stroked his hip and smiled. "It was about time, wasn't it?"

Was this truly who he had become, the sort of man who could sleep with his wife's sister? He got up awkwardly, reaching for his clothes. "I better get back," he said. "I've been gone too long."

He looked back once as he walked toward the dock. She was still sitting there, half-dressed, watching him as he stumbled over the rough ground.

Now he was sitting, perched awkwardly on the lounger beside Maria. Pam came back from the house, her arms full of cans. She tossed them into the pool for the three boys. "Why don't you show me the deer now, Simon?" she asked, smiling.

He looked at Maria. He couldn't tell if her eyes were open or closed behind her sunglasses. "Maybe later," he said.

"No time like the present." She held a can toward him. "Can't I bribe you with a beer?"

Maria sat up in her lounger and removed her sunglasses. He couldn't read her expression. "We'll all go," she said. "Come on, Simon, let's get this over with."

As they walked down the hill, he found himself hoping that the river had washed the body away, but it was still there, fly-covered and slightly bloated. A crow fluttered up from it and away. They stood around it, looking down.

"Wow," Pam said. "That's one dead deer."

He looked at Maria and could tell she was near tears. "Give it a rest, Pam," he said.

She looked at Maria, then at him. "God," she said. "It's just a deer." She prodded it with her foot, dislodging a cloud of flies. "Maybe you should bury it in the backyard next to the hamsters." She shook her head and started back to the house.

He patted Maria's back awkwardly. "I'll get a shovel," he said. "I'll give it a burial."

"Because of what Pam said?"

"No," he said. "Because it deserves it."

"Thank you," she said. She sat carefully on the grass and wiped her eyes. She looked up at him. "I quit my job."

"What?"

"I gave my notice last week."

"I don't understand," he said.

"It's because of George. He'd put his hand on my shoulders or my arm every time he asked me to do something. I thought at first he was just one of those touchy guys, you know the type, but then he started asking me out to lunch, alone. I turned him down after a while; it started bothering me. Finally he asked me to sleep with him. He actually had a room booked in some awful motel out on the strip."

"What did you say?"

She frowned. "Jesus, Simon."

"Sorry," he said. "Why did you leave? Why didn't you tell me?"

"I thought I could handle it," she said. Her voice was shaky. "But I just couldn't work there any longer."

He'd met George a few times; he was smooth, confident, good-looking. He couldn't imagine many women turning him down. "Why don't we sue him for harassment, then?"

"I just want it to go away," she said. "It's not like I won't be able to find another job."

"I know a good lawyer. We'll hang the bastard out to dry."

"Leave it," she said. "Just leave it."

"Fine." He couldn't be bothered to keep the irritation out of his voice.

He turned and walked up the hill to the tool shed by the pool. Through the fence he saw Pam on the lounger beside the boys. Inside the shed it was cool and musty. Most of the tools were barely used, covered with a fine layer of dust. An axe stood propped against the wall. He picked it up and felt its weight, the smoothness of the handle. Then he set it down again with a solid clunk on the concrete floor.

The shovel was old, heavy in his hands as he dug into the damp earth by the river. He had taken a pair of creased work gloves from the shed, but even then he knew he'd have blisters. Maria sat watching him dig. It felt good to be doing something physical; he liked the sweat on his forehead, the warmth in his arms and lower back. *This is real*, he thought. *This I can grasp*.

When the grave was deep enough, he dragged the deer by one of its legs, holding his breath against the smell. It was hard to move, heavier than it looked. He sat on the grass when it was done.

"You need a break," Maria said.

"I'm taking one." He tried not to sound irritated again. "Look," he said. "You don't have to stick around. I'm going to fill the hole. I'll meet you at the house."

She came over to him. "Okay." She bent down and kissed him on the forehead. "Salty," she said. "The sweat of honest work." She stood and turned to go. "Thanks for this," she said. "I'm sorry about George. I should have told you."

He waved his hand in a dismissive gesture.

He filled the grave quickly, his muscles feeling the strain. *I'll exercise more*, he thought. *I've been too lazy. I've spent too much time indoors. Honest work, like Maria said.*

He knocked the last of the earth from the shovel and put it over his shoulder. He took the long way back, past the dock and the woods. They were in shade this late in the afternoon so he almost didn't see Pam sitting on her patch of grass.

"Hello," she said.

There was a strange constriction in his chest. She was cross-legged, looking at him calmly. He could just keep walking. All he would have to do was put one foot in front of the other.

With something very much like despair he put the shovel down and stepped into the woods.

THE FALLEN

The lawyer has a secretary, an expensive suit and a haircut that he must maintain like a putting green. He obviously thinks he's too big for this town, this crown jewel of cottage country, but he's doing everyone a favour by staying.

"Of course the house is yours," he says. He offers me a cup of coffee from the machine on his sideboard and I sip it carefully. I am acutely conscious of the small hole in the knee of my jeans.

"I thought he'd written me out."

The lawyer smiles broadly. Everything is quite droll now that we've cleared away all that unpleasant business. "It wouldn't matter if he had," he says. "The law tends to favour family in an estate dispute. Anyhow, your father's will was quite explicit."

I look at the chestnut tree outside his window. Its leaves are faded and crisp. Behind it, the bright flame of a maple catches the afternoon light. I have a sudden desire for the scent of burning leaves and the crispness of fall air.

"There's a car and there's also some money," he says. "Not much, but it should cover the taxes and utilities for a couple of years." Almost as an afterthought he adds, "Oh, and there's the basement tenant. That's another five hundred a month. Peanuts, of course, but it'll pay for your groceries."

"What if I sell?" I ask.

"Your choice. The market's not great at the moment, but the mortgage is paid off." He closes the folder in front of him and stands up, the meeting clearly at an end. "I think he hoped you would stay," he says, tossing me the keys.

They sit on the dresser in my motel room near the bus station for two days.

The house is full of soup. There are cans and cans of it in the cupboards, stacks on pallets in the garage — chicken noodle, minestrone, leek and potato, cream of mushroom. Dirty dishes fill the sink, fuzzy with mould. Piles of newspapers and magazines form chest-high columns in the living and dining rooms. He made paths through the walls of paper. When I haul them out and bundle them for recycling, the carpet beneath is clean and bright.

An odd life to match his odd death: he'd fallen from the big maple in the backyard. Nobody could tell me why he was up there, at his age. It comes to me, sorting through all this evidence of isolation, that he'd never done anything this interesting before.

Even after my mother left us, when I was still young, he'd kept to his modest, tightly bound life. He would sit in the kitchen after dinner and work on the account books of the small businesses he took care of, humming quietly to the classical music that filtered through from the radio in the living room. I did my homework, wondered at the thoughts he never shared.

At night, sometimes, I would walk around the house and dust, water the plants, scrub the kitchen floor. I kept thinking she would just show up one day. She would look the same, though perhaps slightly apologetic. She would say something like, "It was just a mistake, that's all." She would put down her bags and put the kettle on and sit in the living room with her coffee and a cigarette and tell us where she'd been, all the things she'd seen.

The tenant surfaces as I'm loading the big Pontiac with bundled papers.

"I'm Emma," she says, sticking out her hand. "I'm sorry about your dad." She is in her late thirties, dark haired. She looks like a farm wife.

My hands are full. "Sorry," I say, trying to work one free.

"It's okay. You're Darryl, I assume? Lawyer said you'd be by." She looks at the stacks of newspaper and shakes her head. "It's about time someone got rid of that. I kept telling him to throw it out, but he'd never listen to me."

"He was always stubborn," I say.

"So, are you keeping the place?"

"Well …" I say.

"If you're not, you have to give me two months' notice. If the new owners don't want a tenant, that is. It's in the lease."

"Sure," I say. "I'll let you know."

That night as I sip a bowl of minestrone, I hear her voice drifting up through one of the heating vents. There's another woman, too, laughing with a deeper voice. After I go to bed I can still hear them, their conversation mixed with the sound of a TV. I'm in my father's bed, the sheets fresh from the dryer. Sleep is slow to come.

The house needs work. It won't sell with peeling siding and rotting wood. I spend some of the money on paint, asphalt shingles and roofing nails and start on several potential leaks. I fix the crumbling chimney bricks, filling in the cracks and flakes as best I can.

I'm up on the roof, remembering the times I helped him with the gutters as a child. I have a mouthful of nails and I can feel the roughness of the shingles through the seat of my old army surplus pants. A voice floats up from below, "Don't fall off, now." I take out the nails and lean over to see Emma looking at me from the walk.

She grins, squinting up at me. "Don't let me distract you," she says. "You're doing a great job."

She's wearing a baseball cap and a sweatshirt that says SPARTANS. It makes her look younger.

"Since you're working on the place, could you take a look at my apartment? It hasn't been painted for a while and I've had problems with the stove."

I notice her backpack bears the university logo. "You're a student?" I ask.

"I'm doing my doctorate."

"Really?"

"Yeah," she says. "Really." She wheels a mountain bike from the garage and sets off down the driveway. "Don't forget the stove."

Her apartment is neat. Everything has a place, but it's clear she's not dictatorial. There's the occasional stray. I restrain myself from picking up a book from the floor.

There's a full-scale plastic skeleton in one corner and anatomy texts and a computer on a desk beside it. Against the wall are two large fish tanks, bubbling vigorously. There are photographs on her shelves, postcards on the fridge — friends in far-away places.

The stove is old and has blown a fuse. I replace it, reattach some loose wires, then I sit on one of her chairs, trying to remember how the basement looked when I was young. For years I was afraid to come downstairs. It was unfinished, and half the floor was open earth — a dark, musty scar. My father had talked about fixing it up, but never got around to it.

She has me over for dinner on the weekend to thank me

for fixing the stove and doing some touch-up work on the walls. It's been a while since I've been a dinner guest and I don't quite know how to act. I hang around awkwardly in the kitchen, sipping from a glass of beer until she finally puts me to work chopping vegetables for the salad. "So," she says over chips and salsa, "you're wondering about my friend Stanley." She waves at the skeleton.

"He's *not* real," I say.

"Just a model. Anyway, that'd be rather macabre, don't you think?"

"I don't know," I say. "Some people like that sort of thing." Years ago I dated a woman who had a skull she claimed was Houdini's. She kept it wrapped in velvet in a wooden box. This was the seventies, of course. I found it interesting and kind of sexy at the time. She owned a startling number of candles.

"You're a doctor?" I ask.

"A forensic anthropologist. I don't deal with the living. By the time *I* see them a doctor's not much use."

"I'm not so big on the living either," I tell her. I want to say that I'm glad she was the one who found my father, lying under the tree, but it sounds wrong. It's just that she seems like the kind of person you'd want in that situation. "You don't find it disturbing?"

"You'd be surprised," she says. "You can get used to anything. Besides, corpses don't lie. In that respect, they're far less messy than the rest of us."

Over dinner, I finally ask about him.

"I didn't know him all that well," she says. "I lived in a fleabag old place on Water Street before I moved here. I've only been here a year or so."

"Was he ..." I hesitate a moment, trying to think of the right word. "Was he a bit strange? It wasn't like him to fill the house with junk."

"I don't know if I'd call him 'strange.' Maybe 'interesting' is a better word. He used to give me fish every so often: lake trout and bass he'd catch himself. Wild mushrooms from the woods. He'd never ask for help for anything. He'd even climbed that tree before the accident, going after his parakeet."

"And you don't know why he was up there."

She shakes her head. "The bird was still in its cage. It died while he was in the hospital: nobody remembered to look after it."

After I finish fixing the roof and hacking back the weeds in the garden, I tackle the inside. The cupboards in the kitchen are crammed with cans: spaghetti and baked beans, as well as the soup. The freezer in the pantry is full of bread and the plastic wrapped bodies of several fish.

My old room is filled with boxes: salad bowls, tattered books, vinyl records, wool sweaters, papers, photographs. There's an entire box of photo albums I spend an afternoon paging through. Some of the albums are old, the pictures black and white; all the men wear hats. Others are more recent, full of colour photographs of holiday cabins and children with shaggy seventies' haircuts. I don't recognize anyone. As far as I know, we never even owned a camera, which is possibly stranger than all these albums full of other people's lives.

The records are all old classical recordings: Haydn, Bach, Brahms. He used to sit in the dim living room and listen to them in the evenings. They're dusty, labels peeling; no one has played them for a long time.

This archaeology is disturbed one afternoon by a man wearing a shirt and tie pounding on the door of the basement suite, shouting, "Danielle! Jesus! Open the damn door!"

I stick my head out the window. "Hey," I call out. "There's no Danielle here."

He looks up at me, his face red. "Who the hell are you?"

"This is my house."

"I know she's here. Don't lie to me."

I'm trying to think of something soothing to say when the door opens and Emma steps out. Her face is tight with anger. "Peter," she says. "Go away. She doesn't want you here."

He steps toward her with balled fists and I move for the front door. As I open the door, she kicks him between the legs and closes her own door hard. He folds over and falls heavily.

There are leaves skidding across the lawn from the oak

tree next door. His car is in the driveway, its engine still running. I open the door, shut it off and stand over him.

"Explanation?" I say.

"A minute," he manages, with the strained voice of someone concentrating very hard on one thing. I've been beaten up before; I have a measure of sympathy for him.

Finally he sits up. He's holding his knees, looking deflated. The curtain on the basement door twitches a couple of times. "I need to talk to her," he says. "You don't understand."

"Maybe you should just go home."

"Home," he says. "Why doesn't *she* come home?"

"Maybe you're a jerk," I say. "Kind of looks that way from here."

"Look," he says. "You've got to see this from my perspective. We've been married twelve years; I've got a seven-year-old at home wondering where her mom is. I'm drinking more bourbon than I ought to, following people around in my car. My work's going to hell."

"And?" I ask. I don't feel up to giving him more than a few syllables.

"And maybe I'm going a little crazy. I mean it's not like I can just have it out with the guy, or even say to her, fine, go off with him. I mean, this is something totally different. I'm at the end of my rope. Your dyke tenant there, the one who just suckered me with that kick, she's been messing with Danielle's head."

Things fall into place. "Oh," I say, like an idiot. He

slowly gets to his feet. "You'd better go." The fight seems to have leaked out of him and he gets back into his car.

He starts it up and rolls down the window. "If you see her," he says. "Tell her it's not over. Tell her I don't believe it."

The doorbell rings the next day and Emma is standing there wearing a windbreaker, jeans and scuffed work boots. She's carrying a small backpack. Behind her in the driveway sit a van and a police car.

"What's wrong?" I ask. For a moment I imagine it's about Danielle's husband, that she's being hauled off to jail for assault, or worse.

"Oh," she says, looking back for a second. "Nothing serious. I just have to leave for a day or so to help on a case out of town. A farmer found some bones on his land and my professor is away at a conference, so I'm the closest expert."

"What do you have to do?"

"Examine the evidence. Draw some conclusions." She looks at me soberly. "A fourteen-year-old girl disappeared near here two years ago." She looks back again at the cars. "Listen, I've got to run. Danielle's with her sister for a couple of days. Could you feed my fish for me while I'm gone? I've left instructions."

I nod. "About yesterday — "

She actually blushes. "Long story. I'm sorry to drag you in. Don't worry, it won't happen again."

Curiosity tugs at me like a dog on a chain, but she's down the steps and into the waiting car before I can ask for details.

There's a box of postcards in my old room. I flip idly through them. *The weather is beautiful. Greetings to Helen and George. The people are curious and eat far too much. Marion's been sick for days with some bug.* Then at the bottom of the pile I find a small bundle held together by a decaying rubber band. The writing is familiar.

They're from my mother. Written after she left. I'd never seen them before. I sit there with my eyes closed in the dusty room for a while, the cards in my hands.

The first one is from Glasgow, Montana. A picture of the largest earth dam in the world. *I'm not here alone. You're a stupid, dull man. Look inside yourself to see why I did it. By the way, it's a really large dam. You wouldn't believe it.*

There's one from Saskatoon, another from Prince Rupert and the last from Eugene, Oregon, dated more than a year after she left. They're all the same. She talks about the places she's visiting, almost conversationally, then about his failure of will, his lack of imagination. She mentions her companion again; it sounds like it is someone they both knew. She mentions me only once. On the postcard from Eugene, she writes, *Don't forget Darryl's birthday. It's the 24th of June. You're hardly worth the postage, you know.*

In all my thoughts of my mother — my memories of the time when she lived with us, my imaginary re-creation of her life since — she was never like this. My father was no help; she was a topic completely off-limits.

I trace the curves of her words, the slightly faded images. They reveal no more: there was another man, she despised my father, she cared enough to mention my birthday, but not enough to stay or to take me with her.

Emma's fish-feeding instructions are explicit. She's written the names of all the fish: tangs, tetras, guppies, mollies, angels. They turn and twist through their transparent prison, staring blankly at me from behind the glass. Their food drifts down through the water like snow.

The postcards on her fridge and in a small stack on top of her bookshelf are from friends travelling in Europe and Asia. Some are from her parents, who have retired to Fort Lauderdale to golf and complain about their arthritis and the sagging dollar. No lesbian lust, no vituperative family members.

Why am I still here? I'm the super of an apartment building in North York and my acting deputy, Bob, from across the hall, will probably have alienated half the tenants and found a way to rig the cable box by now. He means well, but it's not a good idea to give him too much leeway. It's a good life there; the physical work is something I enjoy and I borrow books from the literate tenants or the library down the street. I spend most of my nights reading. My life is orderly, smooth, muted.

A key turns in the front door and I stand quickly, feeling like I've been caught in the act.

Emma looks surprised to see me. She also looks tired. Her hair is pulled back loosely in an elastic band and there's mud on her boots. I point at the tank. "The fish," I say guiltily.

"Oh, right." She drops her backpack by the door and unlaces her boots. I stand there awkwardly, not knowing whether I should leave. "It *is* her," she says.

"Who?"

"The girl. The one who disappeared. We haven't got the dental records back, but the bones are those of a young girl. I know it's her."

"Murdered?" I ask.

She bends over the fish tank and taps on the glass gently. "Hey, everyone," she says. "I'm home." She looks up. "I don't know. We've moved the bones back to the lab at the university. Two years is a long time; it's a lot easier when the body's fresh. Then there are the decomposition patterns, insects. A lot more evidence."

"I'll get out of your way," I tell her. I don't want to know any more. "Do you want to come up for coffee and pie later? I was baking this afternoon."

"I had the worst dinner on the highway," she says. "Cop food. Mashed potatoes like wallpaper paste. Try me tomorrow."

I lie on the couch upstairs with the radio tuned to the least classical station I can find and look at the postcards again, but my thoughts keep returning to the dead girl: her bones sinking into the earth, hidden all these years while her parents looked for her face on street corners and news broadcasts.

I used to have a hard time with the news. I took it seriously. I paid attention to all the suffering. My therapist said I had boundary problems. I told her I thought it was empathy. "It's supposed to be a good quality," I said.

"There's such a thing as too much empathy," she told me, expressing it all the same. Perhaps they taught her this in school: the ability to know just how much she can spare before it becomes too much, before she slips toward some dark chasm. So I sold my TV, tuned my radio to an all-music station, set some boundaries.

The next day is beautiful. I do some gardening, clean up some of the debris from my initial hurricane of activity. I find a bundle at the back of the house, covered in tarps.

Under the plastic are sheets of plywood and a half dozen

pressure-treated two-by-fours. There's an unopened bag of nails, a hammer and saw that are beginning to rust. The bundle isn't far from the tree he fell out of. When I stand under it looking up through the branches I can make out a small piece of lumber.

It's been a while since I climbed a tree. Once I make it to the first branch, it gets easier. The plank is less than ten metres up, weathered and faded, crookedly nailed into place.

Geoff, my best friend, and I had built a treehouse up here when we were kids. Geoff was shy and reserved; I was the one who initiated things. It had been my idea to take the wood from a construction site a few streets over. He'd almost pissed his pants when we stole it.

It was nearly finished. I was cutting a piece of scrap wood near the base of the tree when I saw my father staring through the living room window. He turned away quickly, but not before I caught his expression. I knew he didn't approve; he had already told us to stop hammering when he was trying to work. But this look wasn't just one of disapproval. This was something else, something sad.

A week after it was finished, I spent the weekend at Geoff's. When I returned, the treehouse was gone. He had ripped it apart, all but that one stubborn piece, and burned the wood in the old steel drum in the backyard. "It's not safe," he told me. "You could fall and hurt yourselves."

From up in the tree I can see everything. The neighbour-hood, the house I grew up in, Geoff's old place. I used to think I could see Toronto from here, but all I can see now are trees, the slim silver edge of the river, some clouds piling up on the horizon. The world used to seem so large.

Emma cycles up the road, turning up the driveway and getting off her bike. I call out to her and she looks around, confused. "Up here," I yell. "In the tree."

She walks over to the base of it and stares up, shielding her eyes.

"Are you sure you should be up there?" she calls up.

"No," I say. "Hold on a minute."

On the way down my hand slips on one of the branches and I have a vision of myself landing at her feet. If the fall didn't kill me, the irony would.

"What were you doing?"

I point at the lumber. "Investigating," I say. "Do you know what he was building?"

She shakes her head. "Do you?"

"I don't think I'll ever know for sure."

"Evidence only takes you so far. Then all you have left is your imagination."

"Didn't you say the dead don't lie?"

"Sure, but they don't exactly scream the truth either."

I realize she's been at the university all day. "How are things with that girl?"

Her smile fades. "The dental records checked out."

"You don't know what happened?"

She looks down, kicking at a stray branch. "I've found some marks on her cervical vertebrae, possibly a sign she had her throat cut. They *could* be due to post-mortem predation though. Even under a microscope I can't really say. She had money with her, a little backpack. Her clothes were relatively intact."

"Maybe she was running away," I say. "Maybe there was a problem at home. Don't they say it's usually a family member?"

"That's for the police to figure out," she says.

The door to her suite opens and Danielle emerges. "Honey," she calls, "do you want to eat soon? I've made dinner." She gives me a tentative wave and I wave back.

I put the plastic sheeting over the lumber again and take the hammer and saw back to the house with me. As I pass the basement window I catch a quick glimpse of Emma and Danielle embracing. Nothing steamy, just a simple hug. It brings a lump to my throat; for a moment, I want to *be* them.

The feeling stays with me while I look at the old postcards again, eat a quick dinner of soup and toast, marking time.

When I'm moving the boxes from my bedroom out to the garage I discover a hole. It is covered by a square of carpeting, under a box. When I peer down through the hole I realize that it's right above the bedroom in the basement, hidden by the empty fixture in the ceiling. I can see Danielle folding laundry on the bed, innocent, graceful.

Then I remember her seven-year-old daughter. Some of us are in places we don't belong.

"Go home," I whisper through the hole. "It's not too late." She turns around, startled. "Honey?" she asks. There's a muffled sound from Emma, and Danielle walks out of the room. I place the carpet back over the hole.

I remember a good day, a day before things went bad. I was returning from my paper route. It was autumn and the streets were dark. I rode quickly, hurrying home. Our house was illuminated like a cruise ship and I stopped in the driveway beside my father's car and watched through the window. My parents were dancing in the living room, my mother's head on my father's shoulder. They shuffled back and forth on the carpet to the faint sound of jazz.

I was cold and I was tired; it had been a hard day at school and I hated delivering papers, but I stayed on my bike. I knew when I went in they would be just parents again and they would stop dancing and the moment would be lost. But for as long as I straddled my bicycle in the dark, watching over them, everything was perfect.

RING AROUND THE MOON

A week after he tells me he's leaving Canada for good, I take my father to the Gardens for a Leafs' game. We've got good seats — reds at the Leafs' blue line. We sit there sipping watery beer as the players warm up, spiralling like hawks across the pale ice.

"You'll miss this," I say, still thinking the move is something he can be talked out of.

He laughs, a sharp bark. "You think I'd stay because of hockey? That's rich."

"You like it here. Don't pretend you don't."

"But it's not *home*," he says, watching the ice below. Both teams line up for the national anthems and we all stand.

Halfway through the second period, my mind is wandering — I've never been a huge hockey fan and this is a slow, grinding, defensive game. Suddenly my father says, "Watch it!"

I look up as he reaches in front of my face and then I hear the slap as the puck hits his hand. It falls onto my lap and I pick it up, slightly stunned. He rubs his hand then he takes the puck and waves it in the air, grinning at the nearby TV camera.

He flips the puck back to me. "Here," he says. "Didn't think you'd want this embedded in your skull."

"Oh," I say. Rescued again.

He nods toward the puck as if it signifies something. "When I go you'll have to keep an eye on your sister."

"I already do."

"No," he says. "I don't just mean look after her. I mean watch her. Meg's quite a free spirit."

He doesn't know the half of it. "She's lost," I say. "She has no idea what she's doing with her life."

"At least she's taking chances. When I was her age I was travelling around Spain on a motorbike, taking photographs and getting drunk with the locals. I didn't care about my future."

"But you had to settle down *eventually*," I say. "I'm just getting a head start."

He snorts and shakes his head. "A head start on what? Retirement? That's my job now."

Meg calls me a few days later. "It's only five hundred," she says. Her voice echoes slightly over the phone, the sound of the distance between us.

"I thought you saved enough."

"I did," she says. I can hear the tiredness in her voice. I'm not sure why I'm stalling about the money, since I know I'll eventually give it to her. "I got a ride from K.L. to Penang with an Australian and I think the bastard ripped me off when I was asleep in his car."

"What about the police?"

"There's no evidence. Anyway, I don't even know the guy's name — he's long gone."

I'm in my kitchen, looking out at the dusk settling over Toronto. A light dusting of snow swirls under the street lamps. I take a sip from a mug of tea, smell the linseed oil on my fingers. "I'm nearly broke myself," I say. "Last time, okay?"

She laughs. "Yeah, of course."

Last time was in the fall; she called from Pearson Airport. She was back from Tokyo, looking for a place to stay with her new Japanese boyfriend. She canned him after a week and went home to Dad, leaving me with a confused, dumped Toshio, who ate nothing but noodle cups and spoke almost no English. Once he was gone, she took up with an Inuit soapstone carver. Within a month she'd signed up with another ESL school and was off to Kuala Lumpur. The only trace she left was a series of carvings her soapstone man had made — pieces of her body scattered around my apartment as if she'd moulted and left behind toes, fingers and what I fear may be nipples.

"By the way," she says. "I'm going to see an eclipse."

"Oh," I say, hearing the faint echo of my voice a moment later, then the hum of the line.

"Tomorrow afternoon at three," she says. "Sixty percent coverage."

"What are you looking for?" I ask. "What do you think you'll see?"

"This is number six," she says. "Texas will be seven. Seven's a lucky number."

"I'm not going. You know that."

"I'm back in June," she says. "See you then." There's a muffled voice in the background and she laughs. She says something quietly in another language.

"You've got a new man, I imagine."

"Yeah," she says. I can hear the smile in her voice. "Ramie; he's a Malay. Stop worrying about me, Rod."

They're crazy about her, her men. She's always got one in tow. I could never understand it — after all, she's just my sister. She *does* have this reckless energy, though, this intensity. She overwhelms them, guys who are used to quiet and demure women.

I imagine her in the Malaysian jungle with her love-blind Ramie. He's carrying her backpack. They're eating rambutan and mangosteen. Up above, the moon chews slowly on the sun. The locals are banging pots and pans together to scare off the celestial monsters and she's looking through a piece of welding glass, thinking of electricity, of our mother.

I tell her to call soon. I tell her to be careful. I think about, but do not mention: malaria, leeches, viral encephalitis, young men and the diseases they might carry. "I know," she says, reading my mind. "Wear my rubbers; it's raining men."

I do not tell her our father plans to leave us. I expect him to call any day and tell me he's changed his mind, that it was a passing fancy, a twinge of nostalgia.

When I go to Sunday dinner at my father's house in Oshawa he pours me a McEwan's, leans back in his chair and says, "I've put the place on the market."

For a moment I don't realize what he's talking about. "You're serious?"

"Dead serious," he says. "Talked to the realtor last Friday. There's an open house this weekend."

"That's so fast. Don't you want time to think about it?"

He laughs. "If I think about things, I might change my mind." He gets up and opens the oven, prodding the pork with a knife. "I've decided," he says. He stirs the pot of rice, makes a show of checking the cherry tomatoes he's simmering in pesto.

I look at him, waiting for him to turn around. "Glasgow's not the same city we left, you know. It won't be an easy place to retire to."

"I'm buying a pub." He turns back to the oven and takes out the pork. The stuffed tenderloin steams gently on the counter. He looks at me, a small smile on is face. "Something you can't do in Florida. Your uncle Jamie and I are going halves. We used to talk about doing it years ago, back when your mother was alive. Of course, she never let us consider it."

"That's because you'd have lost your shirts. What do you two know about running a pub?"

He finishes laying out the meal and brings our plates to the table. "You're such a wet blanket, Rod. Don't you ever feel like taking a chance?"

"Sure," I say. "Sometimes."

He gulps his beer, then hacks at the food, smacking his lips. "This insurance business is sucking the life out of you." He bends down and tears at the tenderloin like a lion at a zebra. "I need a challenge," he says, his mouth full of meat. "And I need the rain and the hills again."

When we first came to Canada, we stayed with an aunt and uncle of dad's who lived in Etobicoke, just west of Toronto. He told them he was out looking for work, but they knew he was down by the lake, walking. He used to tell me how dark it was in Scotland, how he'd felt oppressed by the closeness of the sky, the dreariness of winter. Canada, he proclaimed, was a country of light and space.

He tromped through the snow in his Wellington boots and an old anorak, his head buzzing with the light flooding across the lake. It poured out of crystalline, scrubbed skies. Maybe his leg and his ribs still hurt him where they'd been broken, but he gave no sign. He opened his mouth wide and sucked in the promise of a new place.

Meg and I had lost our mother, our home, our friends. It was years before I thought about what he had lost.

I worked in claims at Toronto Assurance before they went belly up; now I'm in the graphics and promotions department at Dominion Mutual. I lay out magazine ads, the company newsletter; sometimes I design benefit package brochures for large corporate plans. Once a week I go to life drawing and painting sessions at the art college. There have been layoffs, of course, but it's a big industry. I'm not that worried.

I've been working on a painting for months, a nude based on a woman who modelled for us ages ago. She's in half-light, her body painted with bright strips of sun and shade. My studio is filled with half-finished pieces like this. Every so often I go back to the old ones and work on them.

Meg calls again, collect. I'm hovering over the picture, trying to make the woman's body emerge from the shadows.

"I talked to Dad," she says after I pick up the phone and accept the charges.

"It's crazy, isn't it?"

"No," she says. "I don't think so. He talks about Scotland all the time. He's probably just been waiting until we were old enough to look after ourselves."

I almost say, "speak for yourself." Instead I say, "How was the eclipse?"

"The eclipse was a bust."

"It was cloudy?"

"Socked-in for six days. Monsoon rains. Ramie and I had to hole up in a hut and live on love."

"I'm sorry."

"Fate," she says. "That's why I know Texas will be the one. It'll be a thing of beauty."

"Beauty," I say. "Right."

"You'll see," she says. "You don't believe, but you'll see."

There is a SOLD sticker on the realtor's sign planted on the snow-crusted front lawn of my father's house. It's not a particularly attractive house: a standard brick suburban bungalow with a second floor obviously tacked on later, the usual square of grass and nondescript shrubbery out front. Still, it was *our* piece of suburbia.

I walk around to the back and look up at my old bedroom window, at the deck I'd helped my father build when I was in high school. He sees me from the kitchen and opens the sliding door. "It sold," he says. "Did you see?"

"I saw." I kick at a piece of ice that's fallen from the deck.

"I'll need your help with the packing, that sort of thing."

I stay in the yard, worrying the piece of ice with the

heel of my shoe, crunching it into tiny fragments. I feel slightly ridiculous, as if I'm a kid again, sulking. "Why did you come to Canada in the first place?" I ask.

"Rod." He's peering down at me from the door, frowning. "I wanted to leave everything behind us; I wanted to protect you and your sister."

"Then why are you going back?"

I can hear him sigh; his breath rises in front of him in the cold air. "Because you're adults now," he says. "Because I miss it. Because I can."

"Well, I can't help you pack," I say. "I have things to do. Sorry." I walk back to my car and sit in it with the engine running.

I had intended to be firm, to try and persuade him. He was always stubborn, just like Meg. I saw him as he must look to others — older, unfashionable, tired, in his worn work shirt and socks, his creased, too-dark jeans. Something softens inside me. He wants my approval, but he doesn't *need* it.

I turn off the engine and walk up the driveway to the front door. When he opens it I say, "Fine, I'll help you pack." I walk past him into the house, trying not to notice the bemused expression on his face.

"Shoes," he says. "Put them by the door or you'll be dripping all over my carpet."

Meg comes back early from Malaysia — a week before dad leaves for Glasgow. She's nut brown, her hair sun-bleached to a light blond. She's taken up smoking, rolling small, illicit-looking cigarettes from a pouch of Drum tobacco. We spend a night drinking Dutch beer and catching up. She gave her camera, her Walkman and many of her clothes to the inhabitants of a village she stayed in on Malaysia's east coast. She talks of "the West" and of the real world outside it. She plans to return after the Texas eclipse.

Ramie is history. He asked her to stay, to get married and have children. He didn't understand that there were rules, that there were limits. The poor guy got drunk and crashed his scooter into a palm tree. He spent a week in hospital where she raised his spirits by doing indecent things to him when the nurses were out of the ward.

The night before Dad's flight, we all go to our favourite Italian restaurant. We spend most of the evening telling stories, asking questions about our childhoods and comparing, to my father's embarrassment, the merits and shortcomings of the various women he had been involved with in Canada.

He holds up his hands after we remind him of Lynette, who'd tried to convert us to her apocalyptic Christian millenarianism. "Okay," he says. "Okay. I have strange taste in women."

"Not Diane," I say.

"Yeah," Meg adds. "Diane was great. Why didn't you two ... ?"

He takes a sip of wine and thinks for a second. "I couldn't," he says. "I kept thinking of your mother. Nobody quite measured up."

"Oh." Meg looks down at her lap. I know she still carries a small picture of our mother, taken when she was the age I am now, two years before she died.

"Anyway," he says, changing the topic. "I have a feeling there'll be a few lassies in Glasgow who'll be glad of some fresh blood."

"You're really looking forward to it," she says.

He looks at me for a moment. I give him a grudging smile. "Yes," he says. "It's home. Even after all this time, it's still home."

Meg stays on my pullout couch, waiting for her seventh eclipse. Dad calls a couple of times from Glasgow, excited about the pub, about meeting old friends again. I tell him I'm happy for him.

I come home from work one day and find Meg has pulled out all my paintings and leaned them against the walls. She sits cross-legged in the middle of the room.

"I'm noticing a pattern here, Rod."

"I know," I say. "I have a hard time finishing things." It's slightly embarrassing to have her staring at my work.

"I bet it really bothers you, too, doesn't it?"

"I'm thinking I'll give it up. It's a waste of time."

"I don't know," she says. "Maybe it means something."

"No," I say. "I don't think so."

"Look at them. They're all light and shadow, ambiguous. Maybe you're *afraid* to finish them. Maybe you're *afraid* to see what's really on your mind."

I know where she's going with this. "I'm not you," I say. "There's nothing missing from my life. I don't have to travel all over the world looking for it."

"Thanks, Rod." She gets up and walks to the door.

"Sorry," I say, too late.

As she opens the door she says, "Ever wonder why you keep painting if you're so *happy* in insurance?"

When I was seven I saw an eclipse.

A flaring circle of light replaced the sun, a wedding band in the sky. I looked quickly at it, then worried for days afterward that I would go blind. But it was worth it. As the moon moved, I was handed a small square of exposed film. I held it to my eyes, just in time to see the ring grow a jewel as the sun began to reappear.

We were on holiday on the island of Arran. A small crowd gathered on the lawn in front of the town pub, just down the street from the cottage my parents were renting. Meg played with a colouring book while the adults and I watched the eclipse. My father gave me a sip of beer to celebrate.

Later that day Meg put her finger in one of the cottage's exposed plug sockets and electrocuted herself.

For years afterward, she claimed that everyone in the room glowed with a coronal light, that she'd had her *own* eclipse. But she was four years old when she did it. Who can remember at that age?

I remember the snap of the shock, like a mousetrap closing. I looked over at her. Her fine blond hair stood out in a cloud around her head and her skin shone with a sunburn from the day before. She looked like a small angel. She sat on the floor, perfectly still, and glowed. Then she screamed and my mother ran to her.

The island had no hospital, but there was a small clinic on the east side, where the ferries came in at Whiting Bay. My parents took her, still crying, in their red Volkswagen Beetle, leaving me with a neighbour.

On the way back from the clinic, my parent's car was broadsided by a fish and chip van. My father broke his leg and several ribs. My sister survived without a scratch. My mother was killed instantly.

I sit up late waiting for Meg to walk up the street from the subway station, or get out of a cab, but she doesn't come home. I can't bring myself to put the paintings away. Since moving to Canada, I've left Ontario only once, to go to Buffalo on a shopping trip. Meg has circumnavigated the world twice. I don't know if it's bravery or fear that separates us.

When she returns the next morning, she doesn't tell me where she's been. "I have an answer to your question," I tell her.

"What question?"

"I paint because I don't want to be dull. I never finish anything because I don't have any real talent."

"You're not dull," she says. "You just have to live a little. Come to Texas with me; come see the eclipse."

"Will it change anything?"

"I don't know," she says. "Maybe. Will staying here change anything?"

I look at the pictures propped against the wall. They're not that bad, but they're not that good, either.

"Okay," I say finally. "I'll go, but no hitchhiking and no sleeping in a tent. We'll fly. We'll rent a car. We'll stay in a hotel with room service and a pool."

When she smiles, she looks like our mother. I'd never noticed that before.

In Texas it is searing hot; the air is swollen with humidity. Meg and I stay in a motel full of eclipse freaks, just outside Corpus Christi. There are hippies and amateur astronomers, guys with telescopes and filters and big, bulky cameras. And there's a pool.

We go down to the gulf to watch. The hot air ripples over the sand and out on the water shrimp boats and commercial traffic slide along the Laguna Madre, heading in and out of the city's port. We're almost alone. There are some people walking dogs, an old man searching through driftwood at the tide line.

"What happens next?" I ask.

Meg is picking at one of the chicken salad sandwiches we bought at a deli on the way to the beach. "The moon moves in front of the sun," she says, "and because we came all the way to Texas, we'll be in the umbra, the full shadow."

"No," I say. "I mean, what happens *after* the eclipse?"

"I go back to Malaysia and teach English. You go back to Toronto and make brochures and find another hobby."

"Will you see Ramie again?"

"I don't think that would be a good idea." She takes a bite of her sandwich, a small swallow of Coke. "I broke his heart," she says. "Actually broke it. You should have seen him; it was awful. He thought we'd be in his hometown." She motions to her stomach. "Me out to here."

"What about you?" I ask. "Didn't *you* want anything?"

"Sure, but not *that*. I'm no wife. I'm certainly no mother." I try to think of something brotherly to say and she laughs. "Really, it's okay. Anyway, I couldn't miss this."

Light pours over us, across the flat sand to the gulf. It floods across this wide-open land.

Eventually, a tiny black spot appears on the edge of the sun. It slowly grows larger, until finally I can see a few faint stars and the corona. Then it grows lighter again. I put down my piece of welding glass and look around at the gulls bobbing in the salty wind, the boats inching across the water.

Meg is still staring up at the sun as the last of the moon passes by. Her eyes are obscured by the glass. Suddenly I can see the whole scene as a painting — a finished painting — the two of us on a small hummock of sand, watching the sky, intent on something unfathomable.

NASTY WEATHER

It started long before our layover in L.A., this thing I do with Granite. He doesn't even mind the nickname anymore, it's been so long since the high school gym class when I came up with it. He was soft and pallid and struggled with the simplest exercises. "Paul," he'd try to correct me. But I persisted and it stuck. Even my father, stiff as he was, called him Granite. Of course, he also called him my "steady." I won't forget that.

I push him. It's for his own good. He used to be so timid; he never went out. He's come a long way, though. Now I get him to sit in a dirty L.A. park with me and a bunch of street people for the afternoon, drinking malt liquor and bitters from the Chinese supermarket, cooking wine, all sorts of crummy shit. Then this guy we're talking to, Lonnie, runs out of cash. He only had a couple of bucks on him to begin with, all in nickels and quarters from panhandling, and we've drunk that, so he offers to give me a blow job for twenty bucks.

If we weren't on holiday I might have kicked his ass for that. Instead I say, "Why don't you ask my friend Granite?"

Granite looks a bit uneasy.

"Come on," I say, giving him the wink.

"I don't know," he says. "Twenty bucks is a bit high."

"Sure," Lonnie says. "How about ten?"

"Still too high." Now Granite's getting into it, I can tell. Poor Lonnie doesn't have a clue.

"Five?"

Granite shakes his head.

"How about two, then. Just a couple of bucks?"

Granite shakes his head again. "Jesus," he says.

I pull out a five and hand it to Lonnie. "Forget the blow job, Lon. Just go get us some more of this fine malt liquor."

Granite's still shaking his head as Lonnie shuffles out of sight. "That's low, Dave," he says. "That's so low. Don't you find this depressing?" He waves at the assorted bums sharing the park with us. Tall palms front the road, which I hear have rat's nests in them. Cars rumble by on both sides, filling my nostrils with the smell of exhaust.

"It's *all* depressing," I say. "Everything here is. Don't you just love it? This is why we're travelling, right? To see the world in all its dirt and glory."

"I was hoping for white sand and coconuts."

"Relax," I say, not entirely sure he can. "We'll be there soon enough."

When I come back from taking a leak at the Taco Bell around the corner, Granite's taking a picture of Lonnie. He's standing under one of the ratty palms and flashing his crooked tombstone teeth.

"Step back a bit," Granite says.

Lonnie smiles wider and moves a bit closer to the edge of the road. "Just a bit farther, Lon." Lonnie doesn't catch on, dulled by his alcoholic haze.

"Just a little more," he says. Lonnie steps off the curb onto the road and cars swerve around him, horns blaring. Somebody yells at him. He stumbles back onto the grass. Granite grins expectantly at me.

"Way to go," I say. "Get the guy killed. Jail would be *much* more interesting than Fiji." He looks deflated. "Cheer up," I say. "I got you a burrito."

I offer one to Lonnie, who declines. "Solid food really screws me up," he says.

Before we leave we get a picture of Lonnie, our new pal. "This is it," I say to Granite. "Real life. The grit and grime of the world."

He looks over at Lonnie, at his cracked, grinning face, the duct tape on his runners. "We'll send you a postcard," he says.

Fiji's unbelievably hot and humid. It hits us as soon as we walk out of the airport at Nadi. I get an instant headache. I've been having them a lot lately — they wrap around my skull from the back of my neck, impervious to painkillers. I swallow four Tylenol, anyway, just in case.

Granite's got the guidebook and has our island circled in red for the taxi driver. The trip takes an agonizing four hours, winding through dirty little towns and hills with goats on them. We share the road with donkeys and mopeds groaning with cargo, as well as pedestrians, all equally laden with bundles and boxes. They wave at us, our pale faces peering from the window of the taxi.

Billboards beside the road advertise cigarettes with names like COMMODORE and FIRST CLASS and on each one there's a picture of a white guy in a captain's uniform or a business suit, smiling and puffing contentedly.

Of course, the taxi driver tries to rip us off. Not surprising given the sign on the door that reads AIR CONDITIONED, right under the glassless windows. Even with my head splitting open, I can't stand being taken for a chump, so I hassle the guy, a thin Indian with a moustache, until he backs down from his demand for a surcharge and accepts the agreed-upon price. Granite would have given it to him without putting up a fuss. "You can't let these people take you for a ride," I tell him.

The driver drops us off on a pier, just on the edge of a small town by the water. A couple of kids lean over the railing with hand lines, fishing. They wave and smile and Granite waves back. "Everyone's so friendly here," he says.

"They're probably looking to make some money," I say. It feels like someone's whacking the back of my head with a brick. "Just call the resort, Granite, will you?"

While he's off searching for a phone, I look across the water. Our island rises like a lump of dough from the ocean. I can make out the green and brown of palm trees softening the edges of the hills, the white line of the beach. It's a lot like the pictures in the brochures we looked at in my parent's house, just after the funeral. My mom was buzzing around upstairs cooking for relatives who had come out from the prairies. She didn't appreciate talk of islands and beaches during the wake and I certainly didn't want any condolences, so we went down to the basement. We fanned the brochures across the table, each one a window to paradise.

A few days later I'm face down on my towel, staring at the little pieces of pulverized coral that litter the beach when Granite tells me, all excited, "There's a storm coming."

I look up into the sky. It's blue as a swimming pool. "Doesn't look it."

"A cyclone," he says. "Or at least a tropical storm. It was on the radio in the resort office." Sure enough, that evening, Walter, the Australian who runs the place, comes by the cabins to tell us the storm's due in a day.

"No worries," he says. "This island's sheltered. It always weathers the storms better than the mainland."

I could care less about the storm. I'm fascinated by Walter's leathery face, his laconic voice, the aura of calmness that surrounds him. Maybe I'd be like that if I stayed here and never went back.

After Walter leaves, Granite raises his eyebrows.

"We're staying," I say. "I've been wanting to do this for too long to leave just because of a storm."

"You think it's safe?" Granite asks.

"Sure," I say. "Didn't you hear what the man said? We'd be *worse* off on the mainland."

We wander out onto the beach that night with some beer and some skunky homegrown one of the staff sold us. The moon throws a faint light on the water, the sand, the palms along the shore. Some of the other guests have lit a bonfire down the beach — I can hear one of the young Fijians who works at the resort singing a Bob Marley song.

"You know," I say. "At twenty bucks a day, I could stay here for fifteen years without lifting a finger."

"You're really liking it," Granite says.

"You better believe it," I say. The water is warm. Mangoes and breadfruit and bananas are ripe on the trees. The only clothes you need are a pair of shorts. "I'm thinking of calling the airline and extending my ticket."

"How long?"

"I don't know. Fifteen years."

"It's not like you have a million dollars."

Granite takes out his Zippo and lights a palm frond that's lying on the beach. It flickers feebly for a moment before I kick some sand over it. "I know," I say. "I'm not an idiot."

"You should invest the money. You still have to work, you know. They won't hold your job forever."

"I'm not you, Granite." He's like an old man, reminds me of my father. "I don't have my head up my ass worrying all the time."

"Sorry," he says, "I just think you should remember this is a vacation. You can't live like this." He flicks his lighter a couple of times. "I have to leave in a week," he says. "I have to go back to work. You're coming back with me, right?" He works in a bank and studies to be an actuary at night, as if the bank job wasn't boring enough. He even brought one of his textbooks with him.

"Don't you ever think about quitting? Changing everything?"

"You mean throwing everything away?" He shakes his head firmly. "No."

From the campfire down the beach we hear the song more clearly. "No Woman No Cry," it sounds like. "Suit yourself," I say.

We stock up for the storm, filling the little gas fridge in the cabin with as much beer as it can hold, and buy some more homegrown from the Fijian housekeeper.

During the day we do the usual: eat fruit, lie around on the beach watching the clouds move in from the north, play a little volleyball. The staff run around fastening shutters, pulling boats high up onto the beach, tying everything down.

Granite and I join two English guys we've befriended and take our beers to the head of the island to have a look at the sky. There's a thick line of clouds moving toward us and behind them the sky is green and smooth. Lightning flickers high above and the wind whips sand and water hard enough to hurt.

Granite says, "This is crazy. Why did we stay here?"

"You're scared," I say.

For a moment I see that he is, then he smiles. "Scared we'll run out of beer. Don't we have a party to start?"

"Granite," I say. "You're full of surprises."

The English guys join the party, as do a few of the Fijian staff and most of the other guests, but by midnight it's just the four of us again, passing around a joint. The wind is battering the side of the cabin, threatening to lift it off the ground and send it spinning into the sky. The dank, rattling room shrinks around me.

Finally, I have to leave. "Back in a second," I say, stumbling outside into the night. Trees bend back and forth like dancers in a nightclub, the lightning freezing everything in strobe flashes.

I walk, half-crouching, to the head of the island. Sand and pieces of wood fly past, some hitting me. I don't care. I need to see it; to look up and feel the weight of the storm hanging over me like the descending fist of an angry god.

I sit on a rock at the edge of a nearby hill. It cuts the wind, but only a little. I look out into the leaping surf. The rain stings my raw skin, gusts of wind knock me about. It's more comforting than being drunk or stoned; it fills the spaces inside me. I am erased.

I have no idea how much time passes before Granite finds me. "Dave!" he yells over the wind.

I turn around and see the dark shape of him crouched on the rocks, his hand shielding his eyes. "What are you doing?" he yells. "Come on, it's not safe here. One of the cabins lost its roof a few minutes ago."

"I'm fine," I say. "Go on back."

He shakes his head violently. "No way, not without you."

"Granite," I say. "Fuck off."

He looks at me for a second or two. "What's this about?" he asks.

I don't need this, not now. I put my hand on his chest and push. "Go away." I force him to his feet. "Get lost."

He stands there stubbornly. "I'm not leaving you here."

I can't stand his concern, his continual presence, his dopey look. "You're always following me around," I yell. "You're pathetic." I stand up and move closer to him until we're only inches apart. "You want me to tell you what to do for the rest of your life? You want me to hold your limp little hand? Get your own life, Granite. Get the hell out of mine."

He vanishes into the roaring darkness and I'm alone in the storm.

I'm sure my father would be pleased to know how his money is being spent, his lack of faith in me justified. He'd said as much when he paid me off, a few days before the cancer took him.

He'd called me into my old room, which he'd converted into an office. He was sitting in front of his computer, his IV stand and a cup of pills beside him.

"Playing games?" I asked.

"I'm sorting everything out," he said. "Your mother's useless with money." He was almost out of time. He was trembling just sitting at the desk.

"My will's done," he said. "With the insurance and everything, you'll get about ninety-eight thousand."

"Lucky me," I said.

"I worked for that money," he said. "I worked *hard*. I don't have to leave anything to you. God knows what you and your girlfriend Granite will do with it."

"You don't know anything," I said. "I don't need your money."

He looked at me fiercely and I looked down, despite myself. "I know a few things," he said. "The way he follows you around. It makes me sick. But this is for your mother's sake."

"Fuck you," I said very carefully.

"For your mother," he said. "Not you." He turned back to the computer, dismissing me.

I opened the door. "You'll never know what I do with it," I said. "All those years working *so* hard and you'll never know."

Granite's back at the cabin. Whether he's sleeping or faking it I can't tell. He's curled as far into the wall as he can get without being part of it. I walk up to him, watch the rise and fall of his ribcage, the sunburned back of his neck. Then I fall into my bunk and sleep and sleep.

I wake to a morning that's cleaner than laundry, clouds scooting across the sky at a high velocity. Tree branches and the remains of a boat litter the shore, but apart from one torn cabin roof, the place has survived remarkably well.

Granite greets me with a sheepish smile. "Hell of a storm," he says. "You were crazy to be out in that."

"Mad as a hatter," I say. "You know that, Granite." And that's all we say.

A week later, when it is time for him to go, he looks at me with a strange expression. "Go home," I say. "Live your life." I make the call to extend my flight and stand on the white sand beach watching the boat take him away.

Every day at noon the supply boat comes from the mainland full of beer and groceries and new guests. I sit and watch for it, stroking my growing beard. I'm waiting for the air to change as it did before the cyclone, for one of the faces on the boat to look familiar, for the money to run out.

"Welcome to paradise," I yell to the new guests as they get off the boat. "Welcome to paradise." Sometimes I even believe it.

THE LAND HIS MOTHER

When the redback bit Patrick all he said was, "Ouch."
He sat down across from Neil and rubbed at the spot
below his knee where the spider had punctured his
skin. An hour later he was vomiting in the emergency
room of the Mildura hospital, sweating and groaning as
the doctor worked on him.

Neil had watched the spider crawl slowly through the
grape leaves, fascinated by the careful movements of
its legs, the brilliant red stripe across its black back. He
hadn't spoken since Antonio's truck had brought him and
the other pickers to the farm that morning at dawn and he
wasn't about to start. He was afraid he'd ruin the tentative equilibrium he'd been cultivating — a state of grace,
a vow of silence. The spider, he believed, was a sign, as
was the lizard he'd seen that morning, and the peacock
that wandered the caravan park the previous afternoon.

He squeezed the words out like eggs, new and fragile in

the afternoon heat. "It's my fault," he said.

Patrick looked up. "What?"

He started again, knowing he would have to explain, that there would be far too many words. "You've been bitten," he said. "It might be serious." He saw the spider, injured by Patrick's brushing hand, stumbling through the red soil. He brought his water bottle down on it, hard.

When he handed over the crushed spider in the emergency room, the doctor patted his shoulder and said, "Good lad. It helps to know what it was."

He wanted to say, "No, I'm not a good lad," but he just nodded and sat down beside Molly, the New Zealander Patrick had been seeing since they signed on as grape pickers. "We've been travelling for six months," Neil said to her. "He's never even had a cold."

"This is supposed to be comforting?" she asked.

"We were in a car accident in high school," he said. He wasn't exactly sure what he was trying to tell her. "I broke my ankle, but he didn't have a scratch." He felt strangely calm.

The doctor came out to the waiting room a few minutes later. "No fear," he said. "The spider that sat down beside him didn't do any permanent damage." He paused for a moment, waiting for a laugh. Under his white coat he wore a floral shirt and jeans. "You may as well go. He's sleeping now. Call tomorrow. He should be ready to go home."

The doctor led them to the room Patrick was in. "You've got a minute," he said. Patrick lay there, cocooned in Demerol and starched white sheets, drifting at the edge of sleep. Molly ruffled his hair. Neil stood in the doorway watching them and then turned to look down the hallway at a nurse wheeling an old woman through the ward.

"Big deal," Patrick mumbled. It sounded like he had a mouthful of crackers. "Twenty pounds of pancake mix."

After work the next night Neil got a ride into town with Antonio. He walked into a bike store he'd seen the week before. Inside it was quiet and cool. The bicycles were lined up against the wall, gleaming in the early evening sunlight.

"How much for a touring bike?" he asked the owner. "All the accessories, too — shorts, a pump, everything."

The man did some quick calculations. "I can give you a complete touring package for a thousand, even."

"You can go a long way on that?"

"Sure," the man said. "Had a lad in here last month, he was cycling to Sydney. That's over a thousand kilometres — a hell of a ride."

Neil took out his VISA card. "Okay," he said. "I'll take it."

"Just like that?"

"Yeah," he said. "Just like that."

Once it was assembled and paid for, Neil took the bike outside. Still wearing his picking clothes, he rode out onto the main road and headed for the caravan park. The tires made a humming sound on the pavement. He whirred past farms and fields scrubby with gum trees and grass. His legs were pistons driving him forward.

He stopped for water halfway between town and the park and noticed a movement in the field to his right. He squinted in the fading light. An emu was stepping delicately through the grass. Another sign. It was surreal — the translucent quality of the evening light, the strange shape of the bird. The peeling trees, rusty soil, even the smell on the wind reminded him he was far from home. If he tried hard enough, he could almost fade into the landscape, take on its colour and shape.

Molly was sitting beside the tent when he got back. "Nice bike," she said. She didn't seem particularly surprised. "Give me a ride?"

"Where?"

"I called the hospital," she said. "Patrick's fine, but they're keeping him one more night for observation. He's allowed visitors."

Neil had almost forgotten about Patrick. He felt a sharp stab of guilt; another betrayal.

It had been years since he'd doubled anyone, but after a shaky start he found the rhythm and his balance. Molly sat behind him, her hands loosely around his waist, legs swinging free. He could smell her perfume.

"Nice night," Neil said finally.

"It is," she replied.

The sky was black overhead, softly shaded blue toward the horizon. As they entered town they floated past the faintly glittering arcs of sprinklers, the smell of water on pavement, a trace of flowers.

Patrick was watching TV when they came in. "Hey," he said. "Came to see Spiderman?"

"Sure," Molly said. "Can you spin a web now?"

Neil hung back as they kissed. He looked around the room. On the wall behind him the Virgin Mary stared disconsolately from behind a large wooden frame.

"Neil," Patrick said.

"What?" He realized he'd been drifting.

"No need to look so concerned. They said I can leave tomorrow morning. I'll be back to work the same day."

"Sure," Neil said. "You know, you said some pretty strange things on Demerol."

"I was *thinking* some strange things." Patrick looked at Molly and then back at Neil. "You think you could give us a couple of minutes?"

"Sure," Neil said. "I'll be down the hall."

He sat in the TV lounge with a middle-aged woman in a housecoat. She flipped maddeningly through the channels. "Excuse me," he finally said to her. "Do you mind if we just pick one program?"

"It isn't up to me," she said. "The TV's broken; it changes channels every few seconds."

"Then why are you watching?"

She looked slightly embarrassed. "It comes round again in a minute. You can sort of keep up, you know?"

They watched the screen in silence for a while. He'd

seen something like this in a gallery once; like most modern art, it had made him feel frustrated. He'd felt he was the only one in the room who didn't understand it.

"Hey," the woman said. "You don't *look* sick. What's wrong with you, anyway?"

He was startled by her directness. "I'm dissatisfied," he said, "with how things have turned out."

She smiled. "I don't suppose there's much they can do."

"Maybe not." She looked at him patiently. Was he violating hospital etiquette by not telling her more? "I can't help but feel that everyone else is in on something and they're not telling me what it is. There are rules and I don't know what they are. Things are *happening* to other people."

"Lots of people feel like that."

"Things are happening to you, aren't they?"

"I'm going to die of pancreatic cancer in four months," she said. "Is that the sort of thing you had in mind?"

He closed his eyes. "Maybe," he said.

She shook her head and turned back to the TV's epileptic flickering. "You *are* in trouble."

He awoke alone in the lounge. The set was still on, cycling through static and rugby players. For a moment he had no idea where he was, then it all fell into place. Molly bent over him. Her hair was tangled and her face was flushed.

"Have a nice time?" he asked.

"Sorry you had to wait so long," she said, ignoring his question. "Do you want to say goodbye to Patrick?"

He got up. "Why not?"

But Patrick was sleeping. Neil stood there for a moment, watching him. They'd been friends for years, but what did he really *know* about Patrick? Neil barely knew himself. He felt as if he'd slipped his orbit and was drifting away, leaving everyone behind. It wasn't that unpleasant a feeling, though it appeared to have led to the spider, the hospital bed, the bicycle.

His legs felt like lead as he pedalled down the highway toward the caravan park.

"So, why'd you *really* buy the bike?" Molly asked from behind him.

"What do you mean?" he said defensively.

"We work eleven hours a day. You don't need the exercise."

"You'd be surprised," he said. "It's very peaceful." He imagined himself on an empty road, miles from anywhere, kangaroos and wombats, the soul of the desert.

"I think Patrick's worried about you," she said. "He keeps asking how you're doing."

"I'm great," he said. "Everything's wonderful. I'm having a ball."

She sighed loudly. "Fine," she said. "Forget it."

The caravan she and Patrick shared was near his tent. He lay awake in his sleeping bag, hearing the vehicle creak as she moved around inside. When his alarm woke him the next morning, the sky was still full of stars.

"So, what did you mean when you said it was your fault?" Patrick peered over a low vine, a bunch of grapes in his hand. He had returned at lunchtime, the other pickers gathering by the farmhouse to see his wound. Neil had hung back at the edge of the group, eating his sandwich.

"What?"

"When the spider bit me, you said it was your fault."

"Oh." Neil bent and cut several bunches, dropping them carefully into their black bucket. Antonio's tractor grumbled past, several rows over.

"What did you have to do with it?" Patrick asked.

"I saw it," Neil said. "In the leaves, before it bit you."

Patrick placed his bunch into the bucket. "And you didn't say anything because ..."

"I don't know."

"Well," he said finally. "It happens. Forget about it. It'll be a good story when we get home, that's all." He bent under the vine again. "Remember when we first started here? We'd sing, throw grapes at the women."

"We've been here too long," Neil said. "Why don't we leave? Go to Adelaide or Sydney?"

"You know I can't afford it."

"I can lend you the money."

"It's only another month," Patrick said. "It won't be so bad."

"Easy for you to say."

"What's really bugging you?" Patrick asked.

"Nothing." He looked at the fine scars on his fingers, the red soil ground into his skin. The land spread around them, dusty and flat. "Everything's fine," he said.

When he left the caravan park his panniers were bulging with his sleeping bag, tent, some clothes, a little food and a large jug of water. Patrick was asleep in the caravan with Molly. Sometimes Neil heard them laughing, the sound merging with the small domestic noises issuing from the other caravans — coughing and conversation, the crying of babies.

He took the highway to Adelaide, cycling through gently rolling hills, outposts and gas stations. The road was quiet; only a few cars passed each hour, their drivers honking and waving at the sight of a cyclist, rare on these roads.

Dead snakes and the occasional kangaroo lay on the shoulder, fly-covered, bloated. Were these also signs? He cycled effortlessly, balanced against the pull of gravity, muscles sliding under skin. He felt as if he could ride to the edge of the continent.

He made steady progress, stopping that evening in a dusty town that had no camp site or caravan park. He found a picnic area on the edge of a sports field where he could pitch his tent. His legs felt like rubber and he staggered around like a drunk. He ate cold beans from a can and collapsed into his sleeping bag before nightfall, only to be wakened a few hours later by the sound of whistles and yelling.

When he looked out, the field was lit and men were playing rugby. He watched them run up and down, heard them laughing and calling to one another. When they finished and drove away he lay awake, restless. He imagined he could still hear their voices echoing through the trees.

In the morning, his legs ached, but he painfully packed his panniers, ate a little and set out again. After an hour or so, the ache had vanished and he imagined sending Patrick and Molly a postcard from Ayer's Rock, an image that captured the contrast between land and sky, the eerie emptiness of the desert, the quiet within him.

That afternoon, on an impulse, he turned off the highway onto a smaller road that headed north toward the desert. He had heard there were camels, sheep stations wrapped in solitude. The aborigines had once mapped the land in song — each feature of the landscape a part of a musical cosmology passed on from generation to generation. They had thought the first white explorers were the ghosts of their ancestors. As he looked at his peeling skin he understood what they must have seen. The explorers and settlers, the tourists and all their quarrels and strange obsessions, truly *were* from another world.

He'd only met one aborigine since coming to Australia, in a bar playing pool.

The man had said, "You know all this used to belong to my grandfather? All this land for acres around. And they just took it from him." Neil had felt embarrassed, somehow complicit, but the man had simply shrugged and returned to the game. Now, heading toward the desert, Neil wanted to ask him about his grandfather, about his life, about the songs. Maybe the songs had gone too, like water evaporating in the sun.

He had forgotten to fill his jug at the last gas station. The road was deserted. He hadn't seen any cars all day. His map was useless. When he drank the last of his water, he considered turning back, but changed his mind. He would find something soon.

He had his first hallucination the next afternoon. His legs felt hollow, his pulse was pounding. Every drop of sweat was more water he couldn't replace, but he kept riding. As he came over the top of a small rise, he saw the land stretch ahead of him for kilometres, the road like a thin scar against red skin. Then through the brush, he caught a fleeting glimpse of people running. They were as dark and quick as shadows flickering between the gum trees. Animals, too, moved along the side of the road, dust coloured, blending with the trees and soil.

A kangaroo bolted from the brush and ran alongside his bike, weaving through the trees, leaping forward. He was shocked and exhilarated at the beauty of it. He pedalled faster, trying to keep up, but the animal outpaced him and turned away.

This was why he was here. This was why he had left his home and travelled halfway across the world. The moment stayed with him as he weaved down the dusty road. It remained when he crested the next hill and felt the bike getting away from him, gravity tugging at it like an insistent child. He moved faster and faster, the road beneath him blurred with speed. The sun suddenly whipped across the sky and the Earth took him in her red, red arms.

He was a snake crossing the land like the line of a song. He was a kangaroo, bloated at the side of the road. He opened his eyes and saw pebbles, burgundy soil. The wind pitied him, the sun was an angry father, the land his mother, welcoming him.

He imagined the battered truck that would trundle down the road and pick him up. Its occupants would be brusque, friendly, concerned. They would haul his bicycle into the bed of the pickup and lift him into the cab. They would call him an idiot. They would give him water, salve his wounds, take him with them deep into the desert. He would watch the sun set over Uluru.

He closed his eyes and waited for them to arrive.

FEEDING THE ANIMALS

From the point of view of one of his red blood cells, the molecules that swirl through his bloodstream look very little like the diagrams in textbooks. They are not triangular keys that fit smoothly into triangular locks. They're tiny buzzings, fuzzy clouds, quantum hazes with pinprick centres. They latch onto his cells with a chemical kiss.

Ham imagines the red blood cells as jelly doughnuts, crimson and dimpled in the middle, bumbling through his capillaries and veins and arteries. They are commuters backed up at intersections, tumbling blindly through the body, caught for a moment at kinks in the road.

The blue pill has left a bitter taste in his mouth. His tongue is slightly numb. Its medicine is seeping out, messing with the nerves. He knows it will fade quickly. He's standing in the bathroom now, running a hand through his hair. He drinks the water in the conical glass he keeps by the sink. *What to do?* he thinks. *Do, do, do.*

Ham has not slept in three days. He feels wonderful, though before he took his last pill he did feel a little strange, a subtle shifting in his head. He forgot to blink, then spent twenty minutes obsessed with blinking. To his dismay, it had ceased to be an automatic function. He realized he would have to force himself to blink regularly from now on. Grit would get under his eyelids; he would have scratches on his corneas like a unprotected camera lens.

But that passed, as it had when he was younger, when his body had endlessly fascinated and disgusted him. He'd gone through a period in which he had fixated on breathing. He concentrated on it to the exclusion of everything else, paying particular attention to his diaphragm. He would end up hyperventilating and his mother would have to hold a paper bag to his mouth. "This has to stop," she said. "One day I won't be here and then what will you do?"

After a while he'd become bored with breathing and moved onto something else: masturbation, or plucking hairs from his head, cutting thin ribbons of skin from the calluses on the soles of his feet. There was always something.

He turns out the bathroom light. It's just after three in the morning and he is bored. In his living room, he perches on the balls of his feet, raising and lowering himself. Calves *can* be attractive. This sort of thing would go a long way toward developing the kind of legs he'd seen on a cyclist while driving home from work the day before.

The man had been wearing slick, tight, elastic shorts, a yellow shirt that hugged his lean frame, a helmet with curves like water-carved rock. His skin was dark and smooth. The muscles bulged and released in his thighs and calves and Ham had watched, fascinated, for blocks. He missed the turnoff and had to make a series of detours to get back on track.

He is receptive now, he believes, to the possibility of change. He feels charged — not all the time, but often — with the understanding that he has been given an opportunity to make better use of his time. He is halfway through another exercise, recently devised, in which he perches on the edge of his coffee table, balled up like a swimmer before a race. He finds his balance, feet poised, calves tight, hugs his legs and sways in place, feeling his muscles make tiny adjustments.

Later, he goes out for a coffee. There is a twenty-four hour vegetarian restaurant a short walk from his apartment. It is almost four in the morning and there are only a scattering of people there. The notoriously slow service has adjusted to compensate. It takes fifteen minutes to get his glass of filtered water and to order a shade-grown organic coffee and a slice of raspberry pie. The waitress is young, possibly a student, though without the piercings and chunky shoes that seem to be in fashion.

"I haven't slept in three days," he says.

She nods at him and puts the coffee down to the right of the pie. Liquid spills over the rim and collects in the saucer, but he hardly cares about that. "I'm on new medication," he continues. "It has taken away my need for sleep for some reason. Possibly because I'm a vegetarian, so I'm more sensitive to drugs than other people. What do you think?"

He's not a vegetarian, though she doesn't know this. He said it because at that moment he believed it *should* have been true and because he was a vegetarian in spirit if not in fact, owing to the bacon he is still digesting from dinner.

"You could stop taking them," she says. Perhaps she is thinking of the magazines in racks by the door, their articles about holistic healers, bodywork, various balance-restoring therapies. These magazines are not fond of the medical establishment and the pills it promotes.

"I could," he says. "But I don't *want* to. Do you want to know why?"

She looks at the kitchen behind her. "Not at the moment, no." She walks behind the counter and taps at the order screen, presumably registering his coffee, his pie, his strange questions, in some master database.

Ham pokes at his pie and swirls coffee around in his mouth, forcing it between his teeth with his tongue so it makes small noises. He realizes that if she had stayed, he would have told her all about the inherited skin condition he is taking the pills for. A condition that would, if unchecked, leave him red-faced, flakes of skin peeling away from his eyebrows, raw flowers blooming on the bridge of his nose. Not the sort of thing that would endear her to him.

In university he had used caffeine to help him survive essays and exams. The cans of Coke and cups of coffee invariably left him with a stomach ache and a gritty, distant feeling. His body became a strange appendage he had to drag from place to place. This was different. If he had been asked to describe it — if the waitress had pulled up a chair and asked him what it felt like — he would have said it was like being a crying child, crying until you are exhausted, until you feel flushed out and new, cleansed.

A coffee refill is requested and granted. Ham reads two old issues of *National Geographic*. He cannot bring himself to look through the magazines by the door, to read stories about Tibet and the channelling of wise extraterrestrial presences. The waitress returns. "Okay," she says. She sits in the chair opposite. "I'm a vegetarian and I take a lot of drugs and I'm not especially sensitive to them. I don't think that's the cause."

Ham is pleased. "Why I'm going to keep taking them — " he starts.

She shakes her head. "I know why."

"I'm not *actually* sure myself," he says. "I just have a theory."

"You're interested in exploring perception," she says. "Some substances let us unlock areas of our consciousness we can't usually access. Some reconnect us with the spiritual, things we've lost touch with."

"But it's just skin medication."

She smiles indulgently. It makes her look older. "Yes, it is. It's probably useless for exploring. You should move on to something that does a better job." She stands and straightens her black skirt. "I'll bring your bill."

If she had not left, he would have told her that the reason he keeps taking the pills is because he despises sleep. Sleep is imposed without permission; it is a weakness. Until now, every day for six to eight hours he lay in his bed as the detritus and foolishness of his dreams played itself out. Now he is free of its tyranny.

He pays his bill and walks down to the beach. He removes his shoes and steps between rows of logs laid out on the sand, shelter for sunbathers and crows.

The water reflects the glowing windows of downtown high-rises. Stars are faintly visible through gaps in the clouds. Waves approach and retreat. The smell of kelp and seaweed winds through the air. Everything around him is alive in a web of communication. Trees release chemicals which alert other trees to insect infestation, disease. The ocean teems with viruses which feed on the invisible life within the surf. Intertidal sand harbours minute ecosystems of remarkable complexity. We are deaf and blind and we cannot speak to the world.

For a moment he realizes the waitress was right — our ancestors *could* communicate in ways we have lost. This is the source of our sadness. This is why we cut down trees. He sits on the sand, leaning against the smooth skin of a log where bark has been worn away. The thought is fleeting: what had he been thinking about?

The next day is a Hannah day. He picks up his daughter from her mother's townhouse in Richmond. Before he leaves he asks to use her bathroom. It gives him a chance to look in the medicine cabinet and at the wire rack that hangs from the shower head. There is nothing unusual, though he's not exactly sure what he's looking for — certainly not evidence of another man. He'd be *happy* if Patricia were seeing someone else; maybe she'd stop calling him so often with her fears and complaints. Before he leaves, he takes a blue pill from his pocket and swallows it with a gulp of water.

"My cuticles hurt," Hannah announces in the car as he drives her back over the bridge toward his apartment.

"Oh-oh," Ham says. Hannah sits in the back seat clutching an orange backpack in the shape of a Japanese cartoon character. He doesn't know which one.

"Do you even know what cuticles are?" she asks him. Lately, she's discovered that knowledge breeds moral superiority. Patricia has been telling her things, and Hannah quizzes him constantly.

"A cuticle is a type of macaroni," he says. He glances at the mirror, looking for a reaction. She shakes her head.

"Okay," he says. "A cuticle is a bird that lives underwater."

Another head shake. He sees her look down at her nails, which she's been biting. "Birds fly in the sky," she says. "Fish live underwater."

"That's true," he grants her. "But sometimes animals don't do what they're supposed to. Sometimes animals decide to become something else altogether."

"Penguins," she blurts. "Penguins live in the water." She plays with the straps on her backpack for a moment. Ham remembers to look at the road and takes a turn. "You still don't know what a cuticle is," she says.

"No," he admits. "You've got me there."

Once they reach his apartment and he has taken her backpack into the second bedroom, they have a glass of milk in the dining nook by the kitchen. She holds her tumbler carefully with two hands. It reminds him of the way a raccoon holds a piece of fruit. "We have to go and see the animals," she says.

"Which animals?" He knows which animals. She asks to see them every time she visits.

"You know," she says, exasperated. "The animals you feed with your hands."

He had envisioned Hannah colouring on the living room floor as he marked papers on the imagery of seventeenth-century religious poets — a wade through sloppy considerations of the work of Marvell, Donne, Herbert and the rest of them. He only teaches one day a week, but he is trying not to leave the marking until the day before class. He is aware that he sometimes appears unprepared, that some of the essays he grades he merely skims before inventing a plausible mark.

"We went last time," he says.

"We can feed them some loafs," she says. She puts her empty tumbler down on the table in front of her.

" 'Loafs'?"

"Mom says you have lots of loafs."

"I'm sure that's what she says." He remembers that he has time now, time for anything he wants. The marking can be done in the middle of the night. He is more free than he has ever been.

At the petting zoo in Stanley Park peacocks pluck grain from his hand with quick darting bites. He sits on the grass with his hand held out as they jostle around him. Nearby, a llama snuffles behind the chicken wire fence as Hannah stares at it, fascinated. The peacocks signal to one another with a complex combination of body language and sound, possibly sound too low for humans to hear. Infrasonics. Elephants use it too. Their movements are a complex dance, if only the meaning could be teased out.

Ham lies back on the grass. The September sun is stronger than usual and he feels its heat soaking into him as he watches the visual plankton that darts in front of his eyes. There is a pattern in this, too. Hannah's head eventually appears like a huge blimp easing its way across the blue roof of the world. "You should see the llama pee," she says. Her eyes are wide. "It's like a *fountain*."

After he puts her to bed that evening, after the requisite fussing and glass of water, the careful positioning of the door to allow just the right amount of light in from the hallway, he squats on the floor of the living room, doing his exercises. His legs are sore from the previous night's exertions, but he presses on. The calves of a cyclist are nearly his.

When he is finished, he stacks essays on the table, moving aside the remnants of dinner. They had eaten in front of the TV, something Patricia despises, and in which he therefore takes a great delight. He goes to the bathroom and swallows another blue pill. His face is looking a little puffy, though it is free of flaking skin. He is taking the pills more frequently now; fatigue presses upon him more quickly than it had before. He swirls the tablets in their brown translucent bottle. It's like looking at his dwindling bank balance.

He finds he is particularly sensitive to language — not the plodding words of his students, but the poetry itself, which emerges from the text like a vein of precious metal. He reads, *I was blown through with ev'ry storm and winde*, and can almost feel the gusts sweeping through him, removing the cellular debris choking the gutters of his body. Halfway through the stack of essays he stands up and shakes his head. It is filled with poetry. *But with my yeares sorrow did twist and grow, And made a partie unawares for wo.*

He checks on Hannah, who is strewn across her sheets, snoring lightly. He normally would not leave her alone in the apartment, but it is the quiet centre of the night; the world is still outside the windows. The restaurant is only a few minutes away. He wonders if the waitress will be there. He has thought of her, off and on, about her casual inattention. She has sparked a flare of interest; he's always been a sucker for girls who ignore him.

He takes care to sit at the same table as before. "Hi again," he says when she approaches.

She smiles a careful waitress smile and puts his glass of filtered water before him. "You still can't sleep," she says.

"Still don't *want* to sleep," he says. He's pleased she has remembered him.

"So what have you learned?"

He thinks about the peacocks and their secret language. "I'm not trying to learn anything," he says.

She shakes her head. "So what's the use?" She puts a menu in front of him and heads back to the kitchen. She is wearing black jeans and a black shirt tied around her waist, exposing a slim stripe of her skin. Some sort of Spanish guitar music is playing and he finds himself distracted by the sound of fingers on strings.

"Okay," he says when she returns. He's hoping she will sit down again. "Maybe I do want to learn something."

"Are you ordering?"

He orders coffee and a piece of pie.

"Are you serious about this?" she asks.

"Yes," he says. "Coffee and pie are what I want."

She shakes her head. "No, I mean serious about learning. It's not something to be entered into lightly. You have to be open to the experience and I get the sense you're the resistant type."

"I'm not resisting this," he says. "You know, I haven't slept in more than four days."

"Maybe you need to find out why this is important to you," she says. "Most people like sleeping."

"I'm afraid of death," he blurts. He's not sure why he said it. As with his previous claim to vegetarianism, it's not particularly true. "*That's* why I don't want to sleep."

She looks thoughtful and he knows he has given a good answer. "I have an idea," she says at last. "It will require some trust on your part, as well as thirty dollars."

He can see the swell of her breasts under the black shirt. He imagines going back to her place after her shift ends, cushions everywhere, incense in a carved wooden holder. There will be a mattress on the bedroom floor, maybe a futon. They will smoke some hash and the floor will creak gently under them as they make love in a fuzzy, semi-spiritual haze.

He takes out his wallet and hands her the money. "Okay," he says. "I'm with you."

She holds the bills delicately between her fingers. "Give me ten or fifteen minutes." She takes the menu back to the cash register and taps in his order. She picks up the phone and has a brief chat with someone, looking over at him as she talks. He's enjoying the feeling of anticipation. It's been a while.

When the boy comes in Ham assumes he works for the restaurant. He goes behind the cash and gives the waitress a casual kiss. He must be about twenty, but Ham has a hard time thinking of him as anything but a boy. He has bleach-blond hair, too-long sideburns and a silver stud beneath his lower lip. Ham dislikes him on sight.

The boy grabs a cookie from the jar by the cash, looking around to see if anyone is watching. Ham's waitress is grinning at the boy, who Ham now realizes isn't an employee. The boy kisses his waitress again, this time not so casually. His hand wanders down her lower back and Ham feels his face grow hot. He looks away.

When the boy leaves, the waitress sits on the bench beside him. Ham tries to think of something to say that would reveal the boy's obviously shallow nature.

"Here it is," she says. She puts a small envelope in front of him. It's half full of white powder. Things are not turning out as he had planned.

"This is?"

"K," she says. "It's more powerful if you snort it, but it's rough on the nose. You can mix it with a little hot water and stir it for a minute then add some orange juice. You should trip for about an hour or so."

He is confused.

"You don't know what it is, do you?" She takes back the

envelope and folds it up. "Maybe you shouldn't do this."

"No," he says. "You're right. I should."

She plays idly with the corners of the envelope. "It's called ketamine. It's mainly an animal tranquilizer, but it also has other uses."

"You've taken it?"

"Oh, sure," she says. She smiles a small smile. "ĸ is quite something. It's not like mushrooms or acid — it's good for personal quests, for getting perspective. Just make sure you're sitting down, and have a question ready. Knowledge starts with a 'k', as they say."

He nods. He might ask for his money back. She folds the envelope into his hand and stands up. "Let me know how it goes," she says.

Walking back to his apartment he is acutely aware of the envelope in the back pocket of his jeans. A car passes him and he hears the whirring of the radiator fan, the hum of the tires on the road saying, *You lose, you lose, you lose.*

He mixes the powder with hot water, adds orange juice and sits on the couch with the glass in his hand. He is wide awake. Suddenly he has a vision of himself in the future: going to a rave with soother-sucking teens, popping pills and mangling slang. He is mocked behind his back. He wears inappropriate clothing and tries to be friends with his students.

If he had swallowed the orange juice drink, the world

would have contracted around him. Time would have become a slowly thickening fluid. He would have left his body and become aware of it from somewhere near the ceiling. He would have looked down at his face, blank as a corpse, and understood that he was about to die.

He would have had a glimpse of the relationships that his body has with other bodies: his daughter asleep in the other room, Patricia whom he only dated for six weeks and who didn't tell him he had a daughter until six months after Hannah was born. If he had taken the drug, his mind would have detached itself from his body. It would have floated freely through structures of thought and language, experienced emotions he would not be able to explain later. Then slowly, his body would have returned to him, leaving him limp, nauseous and shaken.

He would have felt a lingering sadness that lasted for days.

Ham puts the glass down on his coffee table untouched. He feels the curve of his jaw; he has not shaved recently and stubble rasps against his palm. He is tired. He can feel it now, the weight of four nights without sleep. He moves the stack of essays aside and clicks on the TV. Perhaps he'll stop taking the blue pills.

When it's finally late enough to wake her, he gets Hannah up and makes her breakfast. He leaves her at the table spooning up flakes of cereal while he has a quick shower. He feels grainy, like a photo that has been blown up at high magnification. When he comes back to the kitchen Hannah is still at the table. She is holding her glass with both hands. She makes a face at him. "This juice tastes funny."

She's drunk more than half of the juice with the ketamine in it. When he grabs the glass from her hand she looks up at him, surprised into silence, though he knows she's preparing to cry. For the first time, he's glad to hear her sobs.

"Good," he says. "Keep crying."

Halfway through the drive to the hospital she sags against him. Her eyes remain open, but her pupils are huge. He is deeply, profoundly afraid. It's as if he has discovered a horrible new emotion. It is the Platonic ideal of fear.

At the hospital they efficiently whisk them into a room and interrogate him while they examine Hannah. He can feel the doctor's suspicion — Ham welcomes it. *I'm a bad father,* he thinks. *Irresponsible, juvenile. Guilty on all counts.*

They take the remaining juice from him. He'd had the presence of mind, at least, to bring it. "You might want to think twice about leaving something like this lying around the house," the doctor tells him. He obviously doesn't believe Ham's story about getting it from a friend to deal with insomnia.

"You can relax," the doctor says finally, grudgingly. "Ketamine is an animal anaesthetic, but it's still used in other countries on humans. Especially on children, as they don't experience the recreational effects of the drug. Hannah will sleep for an hour or so and be groggy for the rest of the morning, but that's pretty much it."

He is sitting beside Hannah's bed. She sleeps steadily through the noise of the bustling ER. She sleeps like a smoothly idling car, like a refrigerator humming to itself. He knows that he must call Patricia soon and that there will be more questions and more guilt and memories that will only fade after months of reminders both subtle and severe.

He plucks a final blue pill from the pocket of his jeans and swallows it. It is the last one he will take. Tonight he will give in to the fatigue that has gathered in him like an oncoming storm, but for now he wants to be awake.

Hannah's eyelids twitch minutely and he imagines strange dreams playing on the backs of them like tiny movie screens. He imagines her red blood cells tumbling through her veins like precious scarlet pillows. They are the most beautiful things he has ever seen.

INTENSIVE CARE

After the Alzheimer's study ended, she walked through the streets with bandages on her wrists.

Victoria saw herself in a department store window as she waited for the bus back to the university. The lunchtime crowds waxed and waned. Her arms were down at her side, held out slightly to keep the bandages from brushing her jeans, her head slightly tilted. She was reminded of the Christ who watched her from the wall of her mother's church, pinned there like an insect. *Father*, he whispered, *why have you forsaken me?*

On the bus, she walked back to an empty seat, aware of glances from the other passengers. She held her wrists carefully, felt the healing wounds throb, the warm flush of attention.

The office was quiet when she arrived. McPhee was at his desk, eating his way through a buffet of paperwork.

He looked at her bandages. "You'd be better off going for the ankles. Tendons make it harder to cut the wrists."

"Don't be an idiot," she said.

He fanned a sheaf of student applications like a card dealer. Snap open, snap closed. "So maybe you were having cancer tests?"

"Did someone tell you that you were funny, McPhee?"

"Heard it before," he said.

She had worked with him for a year and still had no idea if his mocking exterior hid a decent centre, or if, like an apple, he was the same all the way to the core, with the promise of a small poisonous seed.

"Maybe I cut myself shaving," she said.

In the staff washroom, she carefully peeled back the tape that held the gauze around her wrists. The wounds were small and had left a tiny spot of blood on each of the dressings, scarcely enough for one stigmata, let alone two.

They had bought her lunch in the hospital cafeteria after she'd finished — a box of milk and watery spaghetti with a scattering of Parmesan. She'd eaten it alone, eaves-dropping on a group of medical students who chattered about patients and rivalries, doctors and nurses. It took some time before she realized it was a soap opera they were discussing, not their own lives.

She couldn't blame them; the hospital wasn't glam-orous. The tiles on the floor were worn, the paint in the halls was scuffed, the fluorescent lights made everyone look slightly ill, even the staff. She had watched a spider creep across the stained white acoustic tiles in the PET scan room as they fiddled with her crooked wrist veins, trying to get a line in.

Glamorous or not, she wanted a wristband with her name on it. She wanted the doctor running the Alzheimer's study to come back into the room and joke with her. She wanted the technician operating the machine that engulfed her head to tell her soothing things about the gamma rays she radiated, like the glow from a votive candle.

Earlier another doctor — or perhaps he was a technician, it was hard to tell — had led her through a series of tests: placing pegs in a board, remembering a series of words, doing simple exercises in front of a video camera. All this activity with her at its centre.

She would be a baseline, as the advertisement in the university newsletter had stated, a normal comparison, which would earn her a hundred dollars and a morning off work. While the machine did its work she tried to think normal thoughts. "Am I doing okay?" she asked.

"Shh," the technician said. "Lie still."

She could be their poster child, a picture of her lying in this machine, content, with the caption: ALL THIS COULD BE YOURS. People would line up.

In the staff washroom, she carefully put the tape back down over the gauze, pulling it tight again. Despite McPhee, she didn't want to take it off just yet.

At her desk, she folded four of the twenty-dollar bills they had given her into a sheet of blank paper then put it into an envelope embossed with the crest of the university. She addressed it to her mother and ran it through the postage meter.

McPhee stopped by, quarter to four. "You know, they put people like you on suicide watch. Someone to keep an eye on them, make sure they don't put themselves out of their misery."

"I'm sure you'd love to volunteer," she said. "Watching me in the tub like my own private lifeguard."

"Just a thought."

He picked up her envelope by one corner, letting it swing back and forth. "Personal mail in the postage meter?"

"As if you don't, McPhee," she said. "Now let me be. I've eight Ghanaian Ph.D. applicants to reject before I go home today."

The passengers on the bus home shook like bottles in a crate. Buildings floated past like icebergs, dim shapes shuffled along sidewalks. Condensation fogged the windows and she cleared a small hole to see the streaked car lights, the dark mountains lurking nearby. Nobody seemed to notice her bandages.

For dinner, she made a nest on the couch with her comforter and two pillows — a warm place to eat her spaghetti in front of the TV. She ignored the blinking light on the phone, the call display that said her mother had called twice. Meaty, the burly cat the previous tenants had abandoned, weaved himself between the coffee table legs a few times before settling down.

On the table she propped the picture of her brain they had given her. It glowed red and yellow and green, like the map of a lost island, a topography of her thoughts. She touched her bandages gently, curled into the comforter like a cat and let the light of the television become the light of her thoughts.

There was another ad in the university paper early the next week. A researcher was looking for partners of herpes sufferers who had not yet acquired the disease. She stopped by an office in one of the annexes next to the university hospital after work.

"Did you hurt yourself?" the woman behind the desk asked.

Victoria had been hoping for a doctor's office: the glass bottles of cotton wool and tongue depressors, the couch with the paper sheet stretched across it. This office was academic, lined with books. She looked at the gauze on her wrists. It had become scuffed and dirty since the Alzheimer's study ended, fraying at the edges. "It's nothing important," she said.

"And your partner couldn't make it?"

"The ad didn't say anything about that," she said.

"But didn't they tell you on the phone?"

Victoria shook her head. She hadn't bothered to call.

"This is for couples. We're not about to tell women to take care of these things all on their own. There was enough of that with the Pill." She sighed. "Well, we haven't had that many responses. Why don't we get some information from you and, if you're suitable, you can come back with your partner."

She told the woman they had sex twice a week, on average. That her partner, Philip, had outbreaks every two months or so. They had met at a café, she said, where he'd spilled his coffee on her magazine. He'd bought her a new one and they got to talking. She realized as she said this that she was embellishing too much. Good lies were simple.

"So how much does this pay?" Victoria asked.

The woman frowned slightly. "This is a volunteer study," she said. "The hospital does pay an honorarium for some studies, but not this one."

"There are no tests?"

She shook her head. "We're looking at ways of preventing transmission." She looked concerned for a moment. "This is to *help* people like you. There's no cure for herpes, you know."

Victoria stood up. "I'll just break up with him, then. That would be simplest." She smiled apologetically and ducked quickly out the door.

She took the gravel path from the annex to the university hospital. It was soothing, as familiar as coming home after a long trip. The smell of it, the comfort of cleanliness, the forces of order marshalled against the chaos of disease and injury.

She passed the student health centre's AIDS posters and birth control pamphlets, walked past the lobby and gift shop. Plastic signs on the walls read RADIOLOGY, OBSTETRICS, EMERGENCY. When she had been in for the Alzheimer's study she had gone through obstetrics. She had walked past a wall covered with Polaroid photographs of babies, a name, weight and date written beneath each one. For a moment she had thought it was some sort of ghastly memorial. But these were births — life entering the world, not fleeing it.

Outside the main entrance she passed two men gripping their IV stands like long-time companions, smoking. The ground was littered with butts. "It never rains, but it pours," one said to the other.

There was a garbage bin next to them. She pulled the tattered gauze from her wrists and threw it in the bin. The skin underneath was smooth. She could hardly tell where the needles had been.

It's not as if she had been a sickly child. No allergy shots, no broken bones, appendix and tonsils still intact. Visits to the family doctor's antiseptic office did not frighten her, but she did not look forward to them either. Her body was neither a temple nor a burden.

There was one thing, though. At age eleven, she was taken to see her dying grandfather. They had travelled to the hospital in the old Ford her parents had owned for as long as she could remember. The car had no rear seatbelts and when her father turned corners sharply she would slide from side to side, tumbling if she felt particularly acrobatic. Her mother had looked back at her propped on the seat, her legs stuck out straight, waiting for the next turn. "This is important," she said. "It's important for you to see someone before they die. You'll regret it later if you don't have a chance to say goodbye."

That morning Victoria's mother had paused as she rolled up her stockings and fixed them to the garter belt around her waist. Victoria sat on the bed, watching her, the unselfconscious way she smoothed the stockings, pushed the snaps together. "He says he has needs I can't fulfill," her mother had said to her. "He wants an open relationship. Believe me, we all know what *that* means. Open for who, I'd like to know?"

Earlier she had lined the two of them up facing the mirror, naked. "If I had your skin," she sighed finally, "things would be different."

At the hospital her grandfather lay tucked in crisp white sheets, his skin slightly yellow. His eyes were closed. There was bustling nearby, but in the room it was quiet. Beside her grandfather her father sat wearing his good clothes: the corduroy vest and flared tan pants he usually wore only when they had friends over for dinner. His eyes were red.

"He was a handsome man," her mother whispered to Victoria. "A real looker. And he knew it, too. Of course, it caused its share of trouble. I'm sure that's why your grandmother passed so early. The things I could tell you."

Victoria squirmed in the hard chair at the side of the room. She wanted to be somewhere else. Her grandfather made a harsh wheezing noise and sat up straight in the bed. "Get this damn thing off me," he said. He pulled the IV needle from his hand and looked around wildly.

"Dad," her father said. "You're in hospital."

Her grandfather vomited blood, a gush from a faucet, bright red across his gown and the sheets. He convulsed and finally came to rest sprawled across the bed, his gown pulled up so that Victoria could see the flesh of his legs and one buttock. He wheezed again and was quiet.

Her mother grabbed her and tried to put her hands over her eyes. "Don't look, Vicki, don't look." But her mother was the one who couldn't sleep that night and came into Victoria's room to talk to her and tell her how awful it had been, how she couldn't get the sight of him out of her head, how his eyes had been wild, as if he had glimpsed the flames of hell awaiting him.

Her mother called. Victoria waited four rings before answering, looking at the name on the call display. She picked at the remnants of adhesive on her wrists as her mother talked.

"I don't know why he's doing this. Your father and his new-age hippie nonsense."

"Nice to talk to you, too, Mom."

"Oh, Vicki," her mother sighed. "It's one of these spiritual weddings, with that Lana woman, and some witch killing a goat or something horrible like that. They had the nerve to send me an invitation."

"I think they're called 'Wiccans' now. And, anyway, what do you care? He's been in California for fifteen years."

"I *care*. That's all. I just do. And you know how the church feels about that sort of thing. Will you pray for him?"

"Oh, I think it's a bit late for that," Victoria said.

"Maybe you could pray for me, as well." Her mother hesitated and Victoria could hear the faint noise of her TV through the phone. "You could pray that I find someone special in my life, too."

A sitcom's laugh track trickled from the receiver. "I'll see what I can do," Victoria said.

She had visited her father in San Francisco two years before. She spent a few days in a creaking house full of cats, stained glass and crystals. There were cobwebs in the corners, spiders and their tiny bundled corpses. Her father had been taking courses in reiki; Lana ran a naturopathic animal clinic. They used the words "healing" and "sacred" in daily conversation.

"Your mother never understood me," her father told her one afternoon on the veranda. "It's so sad. We've been such strangers to each other. I had all this potential locked inside me, to heal people, to *give*, but I couldn't express it until Lana showed me how."

Could it be this easy? Could she create a new story for her life as casually as her father had created a new family with Lana and the cats and her two grown daughters?

On the bus into work the next morning she stood near the rear doors, jostled by backpacks and elbows. The other passengers hid behind walls of newspaper, Walkman headphones. A teenaged girl across the aisle was talking loudly on a cell phone. "There's no way she'd even think about doing that," the girl said. "No way. Never."

She imagined the bus crashing — everyone suddenly thrown forward, colliding in an intimate tangle of limbs and newspaper and Walkman cords. The phone would be laying on the floor, squawking tinnily as the girl on the other end wondered what to make of all the noise, the sudden loss of contact, the possibility that she had been ruthlessly excluded.

As for Victoria, the x-rays would show broken bones, flaws in the architecture of her body. She would be stunningly stoical. Her plaster casts would be covered with signatures. Doctors and nurses would admit she was their favourite patient.

The bus wasn't moving. "Step down," someone said. She stepped down and the doors opened to the university bus stop where she was borne out on a wave of backpacks and fleece.

When she got to the office, McPhee's cubicle was unoccupied. She flipped quickly through the university directory, leaned into the phone.

The secretary on the other end was confused. "You've got the wrong department," she said. "You'll have to talk to HR."

"No," Victoria said. She looked around to make sure her co-workers were elsewhere. "I'm looking for studies, tests, that pay the participants."

"Ah." There was a pause, a shuffling of papers. "Are you a student at the university?"

"Yes," she replied without hesitation.

"At the moment, we pay an honorarium to healthy volunteers for spinal taps and rectal exams. Practice for the medical students. It's fifty dollars for a spinal tap and twelve an hour for rectal exams."

Victoria thought about the hospital, imagined herself lying on a bed as students and doctors hovered over her.

"Sweetheart," the woman said, reading her silence as hesitation. "I really wouldn't recommend either. Better to ask your parents for money than be a guinea pig. Some of them can barely tie their shoes and you want them punching holes in you?"

"But people *do* sign up for this?"

"People sign up for *everything*. They even sign up for phase one clinical trials and God knows what those involve."

They involved this, principally: testing the safety, dosage range and side effects of new drugs before their use on sick patients to see if they actually do the things the drug companies want to advertise in brochures and tasteful TV commercials.

And the next trial, due to start in twelve days, involved an honorarium of eighteen hundred dollars to be paid on the final day of the fourteen-day in-patient trial.

The doctor's name was Harold. She didn't catch the psychologist's name.

"Any pre-existing medical conditions?" Harold doodled on the lined pad of paper on the desk in front of him. He drew mountain ranges and clouds. He drew what looked to be small cars with angry people driving them. The psychologist sat balanced on the back two legs of his chair.

"Didn't I put that down already?" Victoria asked.

Harold's face gathered itself into a pinched expression. "This is a legal requirement. 'We the undersigned, do concur that subject X is competent both physically and psychologically to undergo the following phase one clinical trial.' It's part of the process, along with the tests, your medical history and the informed consent form."

Harold drew what looked to be a snake swallowing its tail. Round and round we go. He asked her some other questions and she realized that he was reading random sections of the medical history she had filled out the day before. No, she has never had drug allergies, nor a period of depression, nor compulsive behaviour, nor medication to treat a chronic condition, mental or otherwise.

He finished and flipped the form over, making a quick note on his pad. He pointed a finger at the psychologist. "Off you go."

The psychologist leaned forward. "Would you characterize yourself as a risk taker?"

"It feels like I'm applying for a job," she said.

"You are, essentially. A job with risks. One that doesn't pay a great deal of money. So, we'd like to have an idea of your motivation."

"Screening out the weirdos," she said.

"Everyone has a story," he said diplomatically, rocking back on the legs of his chair. "Some are more fit than others."

The trial application had seemed inevitable when the secretary had told her about it, as inevitable as eating, as falling in love. Not that her motivation was love, but it was *like* love. It had certain things in common.

"Most candidates — " the psychologist started. He looked sympathetic. "Most say something about wanting to help other people, the advance of medical science. Sometimes they say they want the money, but that's not really what we want to hear."

The thing about love wouldn't fly, wouldn't come out right. The two men would look at her and they would place her in the company of the unfit. "I want to help medical science," she said. "Other people. To make the world a better place."

They smiled and nodded and made their notes.

She loved the needle, its fine, fine tip. It dipped into her like a mosquito, scarcely a whisper of pain. It pulled blood from her veins, darker than wine.

She loved the way the nurse swabbed her skin first, the way she was measured and tested and tested again: urine samples, stool samples, the prevalence of T helper cells. They tested her coordination and her balance. Her scores were excellent.

The high windows let in bright squares of light that slid across the floors, the beds, the other participants in the trial. Galaxies of dust spun slowly.

"You're glowing with health," one of the nurses said on her second day. Everyone was on low doses; there were no apparent side effects. "Not something we're used to in here."

That night she lay awake and listened to the creaking beds, muttering, sighing, the various noises of the hospital. Next door the machines of the ICU beeped out short syllables of love. *Still beating*, they murmured. *Still beating*.

They played board games, long sessions of Monopoly and Risk, Scrabble, chess, anything with cards. The games and the decks were worn, the Monopoly money as soft and tattered as cloth. There was a TV in the waiting room next door to the ICU. They shared it with the families of the intensive care patients. She found herself fascinated by these tired people, some visibly shaken by the tragedies that had brought them here, others blank and silent. All waiting, waiting.

Some of the other trial participants invented diseases and symptoms when they were sharing the room with these families. They bantered back and forth about their kidneys, about terrible accidents, the virulent diseases they might be carrying. She couldn't tell if they were mocking, or if they were simply trying to justify their presence, claiming kinship with the real patients outside the door.

Don, a lapsed student, was the worst. He and Victoria were sitting on the couch in their pyjamas. A man and a woman in their late thirties were there, parents, perhaps, awaiting the verdict on their child.

"When do they take them off?" Don asked her.

"This isn't a good idea," she said. She glanced at the couple in the chairs beside them.

"Above the knee or below?" he asked. His face was grave, concerned. "Though I suppose that depends on how far the gangrene has travelled, doesn't it?"

She looked at her legs. "You've mistaken me for somebody else," she said.

"Vicky, Vicky," he said. "No use avoiding the truth, is there?"

She stood up and pushed the door open. "Fine," he called

after her. "But I don't want to be the one to tell our kids."

The ICU was peaceful, its residents all asleep or unconscious. A child of twelve or so lay in the nearest bed, so pale she could hardly believe there was any blood left in him. She sat in the chair by his bed. He was as still as the air in a shuttered room, the furniture covered in sheets.

Side effects may include: fatigue, flu-like symptoms, nausea, vomiting, diarrhoea, loss of appetite, flaking skin, oedema, rashes or redness, dizziness, sudden blood pressure changes, insomnia, anxiety, depression, dry itchy eyes.

Side effects may also include: boredom, restlessness, irritability, a growing hatred of board games (including but not limited to Risk, Clue, Pictionary, Scrabble), transient but repeated conversations about life and its meaning, romantic entanglements of a confusing nature.

Adam has done this before. "Really?" she asked.

"It was a bacterial vaccine test. Two weeks in the hospital, like this one."

"Did it pay well?" Don asked, sunk deep into a faded lounger. Beside him two chess players, oblivious, were locked in battle like rutting stags with entangled antlers.

Adam has dark hair that has taken on a life of its own. A small smile. "It was supposed to be two grand. Most of us got pretty sick, though. They ended the trial early when it was obvious the vaccine was almost as bad as the disease. So they only gave us half the money."

"They better not try that here," Don said. "I'm sticking this out to the end, no matter what."

"That's what I thought until I got sick."

"But you're back to try again," Victoria said. "There must have been something."

Don laughed. "Eighteen hundred somethings, sugar. Don't underestimate the persuasive power of cash."

This was the first day of side effects. The doctors and nurses have been busy. "I know you *feel* nauseous," she had heard one say. "But how would you rate it on a scale of one to ten?"

Victoria toyed with the Monopoly set's pewter top hat. "You're not here for the money," she said to Adam.

"Everyone's here for the money," Don said, "no matter what they say."

"What else would it be?" Adam looked at her.

"Something else," she said. "Maybe something else."

The side effects don't knock on the door, they knock it down. She woke in the middle of the night from a feverish dream. Her body ached, her head was pounding. The rest of the night was a blurring of half-sleep and restless squirming. At some point she heard a voice say, "Jesus Christ."

The nurse scolded her in the morning. "There's a call button," she said. "Let us know if you're sick; that's what we're here for." The nurse had a clipboard. "So, would you call these symptoms flu-like?"

"Yes," Victoria said, trying not to be sick over the clean sheets and the nurse's white sneakers. "Yes, I would."

The nausea ebbed late in the morning, helped by some Tylenol and some other pills, chilled water and soda crackers. It was what she imagined pregnancy might be like, as if her cells were shifting into a new configuration.

The woman in the bed beside her had a beet red face. She held up her hand and peeled off a thin strip of skin. "It's like some weird science fiction movie," she said to Victoria. "I'm a pod person."

Adam stopped by. "Feel like some TV?" There were faint traces of redness on his skin, a touch of embarrassment if you didn't know better.

The room tilted when she got out of bed. She felt his hand on her shoulder. "Careful." She closed her eyes and the dizziness passed. His hand remained for a few moments.

"I'm fine," she said.

The soap opera people controlled the TV. "You can sit on the floor," someone said, but Victoria and Adam stood in the doorway. On the screen a man with a moustache drove away from a mansion.

"Come on," she said. "I know where we can go."

She led him into the ICU. The pale child was gone. She didn't know if this was a good thing or a bad thing. A woman was there in his place. There was a faint bluish cast to her face, dark circles under her eyes. "This is cheery," he said.

She was going to tell him something about the peace she found there. She felt he would understand. But there were people around: doctors, nurses, a small clutch of students. A nurse came over to them. "I know you're with the drug trial," she said, "but you can't just wander all over the place. Go back to your ward. Go make your money."

"Some of them don't like us," Adam said as they left. "Obviously."

They sat carefully by the games table. Her skin prickled slightly. She was acutely aware of each square inch of it, of the rough fabric against the backs of her arms.

"People lie," he said. "I saw druggies covering stuff up at the last trial, a guy who actually managed to hide needle marks. They caught him going through a supply cabinet one night. It's a lot of money for some people."

"For you?"

"I'm a musician," he said. "This gives me time to work."

"Pincushion time," someone called out. The nurses were coming with their needles and cotton wool and absolution.

Skin flaked from the joints of her fingers and toes, from the backs of her hands. The woman in the bed beside her had moved onto fatigue and loss of appetite, at least that's what Victoria surmised from the listless way she pushed

Jell-O around on her breakfast plate.

"Come on." Don and Adam were standing beside her at the games table. She was sipping the last of her weak herbal tea. They were wearing regular clothes.

"Giving up?"

"It's the weekend. We deserve a break," Don said. "The student union pub opens in fifteen minutes and we have three hours before we're tested again."

She glanced around. The room was nurse-free. "Totally against the rules, of course."

"Of course," Adam said. "Street clothes are in boxes in the changing room."

The pub was nearly empty save for a few football fans slouched in front of the TV. She fingered the hospital bracelet on her wrist. Don and Adam bought a jug of beer and returned with three glasses, some peanuts. She thought about checking her voice mail, the neighbour who was watching the cat. It seemed like an enormous effort. The peanuts were salty. She gently cracked them with her teeth, feeling their oily slickness. Don and Adam were talking about bands, about basketball, about other things she found uninteresting.

The beer made her feel bloated and slightly dizzy. They bought a second jug. She played with the peeling skin on her hands. "I'm heading back," she said after a while. She got up. "Not that you're not a charming pair to play hooky with."

Adam stood up. "I'm done, too," he said.

There was still half a jug left. Don looked at them, looked at the beer. "Pussies." He looked sour. "I'm not going to let this go to waste. Off you go. Don't be late."

"Let me show you something," Adam said. He led her toward the edge of campus. Leaves were accumulating and were carried upward by gusts of wind. They came upon rows of whitewashed greenhouses, wooden buildings. "This is Botany," he said. "I had a girlfriend who worked out here, taking care of the plants."

"Had," she said.

He glanced at her. "It was a while ago."

He led her to the back of one of the greenhouses. There was a door with a push-button keypad under the handle. He tapped out a quick combination and the lock clicked.

Inside was an explosion of green: palm fronds, ferns, humid air that smelled of soil and chlorophyll. They sat on a wooden bench near some bags of aggregate and compost, what looked to be a banana tree.

"It's fabulous," she said.

He leaned toward her with a look in his eyes. "I'm older than you," she said. She felt nervous.

"So?"

"And this trial is an artificial environment. We're all full of drugs and boredom. It'll wear off."

He rubbed a banana leaf between his fingers. "*This* is an artificial environment. It just speeds up what's already there, waiting to grow."

"You're a boy," she said. "Do you think you have the patience for someone like me?"

He leaned over and kissed her. He tasted of beer and peanuts. She felt something shifting inside her; her feet tingled. She thought she should tell him this. He would think it was some sort of sign and, who knew, maybe he would convince her it was.

She reached down to rub her ankle and found it puffy, swelling beyond the sides of her shoe. She lifted up the leg of her pants and Adam touched the skin there, leaving a mark that faded like breath on a mirror.

"I think maybe this is a side effect."

He took her hand and pulled her to her feet. "Oh, that's a side effect all right," he said.

In very little time, her legs had swelled so much that her pyjama trousers no longer fit and she had to wear a hospital gown. Her legs were red and blotchy, sausages barely fitting their cases. Her hands couldn't fasten her buttons and the nurses had to cut off her rings. The lead doctor on the trial stood beside her bed. "A moderate case of oedema," he said. "You shouldn't worry too much about that. What we've got to look out for is something called 'capillary leak syndrome.' That can be problematic."

"You're stopping my drugs," she said.

"We're stopping everything in your case." He wrote

something on her chart. "You're not out of the woods yet, you know."

Things became less clear to her. Breathing was not as easy as it once was. A nurse injected her with something. The doctor said something about her heart. She could feel it talking to itself in her chest, using small words, speaking quickly. Time passed. The light faded from the high windows and people spoke in quiet voices. She was taken to a different room. There were tiny red eyes blinking in the darkness and soft beeping.

She was making this sacrifice all alone. The doctors and the nurses could no longer bring comfort. Everyone had left her. She felt warm tears on her cheeks, a tightness in her throat.

Victoria dreamed she was in her bedroom with a case of the measles. She had lost her voice and her mother had given her a tin whistle to summon her. She blew a small tune and her mother climbed the stairs to her room. Perhaps she wore an apron, flour dusting her cheeks. On a tray a bowl of mushroom soup with the crackers broken into it, a glass of ginger ale stirred until it was free of bubbles, a *National Geographic*, fresh from the mail.

Her mother sat with her, holding her hand, for as long as Victoria needed her.

It grew lighter in the room. She became aware that Don and Adam were standing by her bed in the intensive care unit. Adam's face was redder, his hair wilder. Don was untouched.

"How are you so lucky?" she asked him.

"It's good to hear you talk," Adam said. "People were worried about you."

"One person in particular," Don said. "Holding your hand half the night long."

"How are you so lucky?" she repeated, looking at Don's clear, guileless face.

"I'm surprised nobody else is doing it," he said. He was grinning.

It dawned on her. "You're not taking the drug."

"Close," he said. "I've been keeping a low dose, ditching half my meds down the toilet. I told you I'd last this trial out. Unlike yourself ..."

He was still grinning and she realized she didn't particularly care. "Go," she said. "Go make your money."

Adam remained. He sat in the plastic chair beside her. "You should see yourself," he said. "You look like a hundred bucks."

"You really don't know what you're getting yourself into," she said.

"Who does?"

HEART OF THE LAND

Before I travelled into the north I lived in a small apartment in the suburbs. I was not working any longer, so I walked down to Lake Ontario every morning and fed the Canada geese. I moved slowly through the forest of their undulating necks, sowed bread among them and listened to their plaintive honking. During the day I ate soup from cans and made phone calls and wrote letters to people who were embarrassed to hear from me. The hospital wouldn't even let me pass through its doors.

Before I lived in the apartment, I had a condominium at Harbourfront, facing away from the Gardiner, out to the lake and the small tufts of island anchored before the city. I cycled the paths beside the water on mornings I wasn't working or on call and ate breakfast looking across the water. In winter I walked. I loved the way the lake changed with the seasons: the glitter it had in summer when sails skimmed across it; the grey cast it took on in autumn when the wind ruffled it; the cleanness of snow on ice in winter, broken only by the shimmering trails of the island ferries.

Water has always calmed me, though I have never learned how to swim. When I was a child it was all I would drink and this calmed me too — glass after glass of it, cold, straight from the tap. I never developed a taste for soft drinks or milk, though my mother tried for years to change this. Now that I am up north, canoeing, I drink water with iodine tablets in it, mixed sometimes with Gatorade crystals to keep my electrolytes up. I must be swallowing two or three litres a day.

When I lived in the city my job was to open people's heads and look inside. Sometimes I removed cancers the size of golf balls, sometimes portions of the brain itself — knots of tissue that had rebelled or were issuing conflicting orders. Once I put an electrode directly on the surface of a man's brain, right at the speech centre, and he said, "Fuck your mother," in a clear, precise voice. I moved it a millimetre and he said, "Problematic." Then he said, "Pop, pop, pop," until I removed it. I wanted to keep moving it to see what else he might say. Perhaps something profound was waiting inside him to be awakened by a spark.

I did not know then that my life was perfect. It was perfect the way the harbour is perfect in winter, when it has frozen and the snow has just stopped falling. Of course, there is still water moving darkly underneath, toxins in the sediments, and the ferries soon carve their tracks across it. But for that brief time it has no flaws.

The first time I saw Susan she had a Medusa tangle of wires writhing out from her head. There were no cards or flowers beside her bed; she seemed to be without family or friends. No one took her hand; no one sat and talked to her as people often did to the comatose.

Wayne, a colleague of mine, almost a friend, called me in to have a look at her. She lay pale and motionless. The wires led to a cluster of computers beside her. Bright lines moved rapidly across a set of display screens.

"I'm in a hurry," I said.

"Stay a minute," he said. "I think this will interest you." He pointed to one of the screens. "Remind you of anything?"

The lines had the bumpy look of REM sleep. "Looks like an EEG of someone dreaming."

"Right," he said. "But she's comatose. She's got a brain tumour. There's not supposed to be so much activity in a comatose brain, not in her state."

"So that's why she's wired up?"

He nodded. "Partly. We're also trying something new. We're trying to read her mind."

I looked at him, waiting for the punchline, but he simply nodded. "Seriously. We're not *actually* reading her thoughts, but we've got an electrode grid over her Broca's area. If she *is* dreaming, she might vocalize something. I'm hoping that with the computers we'll be able to translate the electrical patterns into speech."

I looked at her again, frail and threatened under the wires and the blanket. "How did you get authorization?" I asked.

"She's got no family, no guardian." He shrugged. "She's going to die soon, anyway. The ethics board finally said it was okay, as long as we weren't invasive."

What confidence we had! The heart was a pump, the liver a sieve, the brain a soft computer. With a stroke of the keys, all its secrets would come tumbling out.

The next day I performed an eight-hour cancer operation. Afterward, Delores, the scrub nurse pulled out a photograph. It was a graduation picture, a woman in her early twenties. Her hair rose in a blond cloud over her head. "She's my cousin," Delores said. "A teacher. What do you think?"

Delores was always mothering me, bringing food, winter scarves and pictures of various female relatives. "Delores." I smiled at her. "You know I'm married to my job."

"You've never even met her."

I peeled off my gown and dumped it in the bin. "Maybe when I finish my residency. I'll have more time then."

She shook her head. "All the good ones will be gone, you know."

I went up to Neurology and looked in on Wayne's patient. One of his medical students was there typing something into the computer. The woman lay still, the sheets like snow over the landscape of her body. Watching, I finally saw the gentle movement of her chest.

"Can I help you?" the student asked. I'd been standing at the doorway, lost in thought.

"Sorry," I said. "Just curious. Tell Wayne I stopped by."

That night I sat at my dinner table eating microwaved pasta, trying to read a new journal. I found myself looking out across the water, thinking of the comatose woman, the machines that were trying to eavesdrop on her thoughts. It seemed indecent.

I was dozing, coming off the end of a long shift. I had sore eyes from looking through the operating microscope, an aching back from standing all day. I dropped into a chair in Susan's room to watch over a new program the computers were chewing through, a favour for Wayne while his students were busy. The sound of beeping woke me. When I tapped gently on the computer's keyboard I heard a voice whispering from the speakers. "Don't worry," it said. "I'm changing. Go down to the beach."

She lay there unmoving, still as water. Her voice wound through the air like smoke and I watched her. "Leaves," the voice said. "Leaves everywhere." She must have sensed autumn in the air. "The sky is dark today. And that's smoke on the wind. Can't you smell it? I think the fires are coming closer."

Wayne had been using software evolution to examine her, running through hundreds of different programs a week to find one that would work. If I marked this one down as a failure, they would move on and perhaps never succeed. It would be a strange, reckless thing to do, but it would end this eavesdropping, this exposure. I looked over at her wan face.

I carefully copied the successful program to a disk and then told the computer it had failed, that it should try another.

As I prepared to shut down the system she spoke again. "When you took me away," she said, "why did you leave me there? Where's everyone else?" It was so hard not to reply, to leave her there in silence, locked in her skull.

It was late, a few nights later, the halls were quiet and I was tired and a little depressed about a long operation that hadn't gone well. Wayne's project was still running, the computer humming uselessly beside her bed, no longer a conduit for her words. Suddenly I understood: I could be a witness. I could be there for her.

Nights when I had finished working and should have been sleeping in my condo by the cold face of the lake I sat in Susan's room, listening to her dreams. I told Wayne I was interested in his project. I told him I'd monitor his equipment when neither he nor his assistant were there. All I did was load in my program and listen to her voice, watch her still face and imagine her lips moving in speech.

Almost without thinking, I began to talk back to her. Just murmurs at first, but the more I spoke, the more it felt as if we were actually communicating. One night she said, "Will you swim with me?"

"Of course," I said.

She hummed a tune for a few seconds. "The water is so beautiful." Then, "Where are you?"

"Beside you."

"Isn't the water beautiful?"

I sat on the edge of the bed and held her hand. It was warm, full of life. She didn't move, but she said, "It's beautiful." She said, "Nice." She said, "Where are you?"

The next night she said, "Tell me something true."

I told her about my childhood, how I had been shy and clumsy and spent all my time indoors. I talked about my condominium and the expensive kitchen equipment I'd never used, the way the lake looked under bruised autumn skies. I told her things I had never thought about before. Sometimes she said, "Tell me something true," and sometimes she said, "Peter, come back to bed," or "Why are you like that? You look sad."

I held her hand, watched the rivers of blood under her translucent skin, the blue in her wrists startlingly bright. I read her charts, examined her CAT scans, the MRI images that glowed from the hospital computer. Inoperable, they said, no matter how often I stared at them. Inoperable.

Susan's tumour grew larger and more and more frequently the EEG showed the deep, slow waves of true coma. Wayne started winding down the project and told me I didn't need to help any longer. But I couldn't stop visiting her room. I tried, but when I didn't go for three days, I became anxious and worried. I imagined she'd died, that no one had been with her; perhaps she'd had a message for me and it had gone unheard.

To evade Wayne, I began coming in after midnight. She talked less frequently, but she still talked, if I waited long enough. I stopped reading my journals and takeout containers piled up in my garbage.

One day during an operation I fell asleep. I was working with another surgeon and as he continued I closed my eyes and let my head rest against the microscope. I woke with a jerk when he said my name. "Sorry," I said quickly. "Thinking about something else."

He looked at me seriously. "You're not an intern anymore," he said. "Get a full night's sleep before an operation or don't bother coming in."

Delores came up to me afterward. "Are you okay?" she asked.

"Sure," I said. "I'm fine."

"I'm meeting my cousin for a bite; why don't you come along? Maybe it'll perk you up."

I looked at my shoes. There was a small spot of blood on one of them. I wiped it carefully against my pants. "Okay," I said.

Her cousin was already sitting in one of the booths at the restaurant across the street. She was the woman from the picture, the one with the cloud of hair. Her name was Mary and she taught third grade.

"So," she said. "You're the brain surgeon."

"I'm a neurology resident, actually."

"Oh." She looked sheepish.

I felt sorry for her for a second. "It's almost the same thing," I said. "I'll be a brain surgeon when I finish."

We ate, but they did most of the talking. They went on about Mary's students. I could hardly pay attention. I finished my overcooked burger and watched them for a while. Mary seemed nice enough, but she didn't compare with Susan.

On the way back to the hospital, Delores said, "She likes you, you know."

For a moment I felt confused, unsure whom she was talking about.

"Mary asked if you wanted her phone number."

"Her number?"

Delores shook her head. "So you can call her. So you can ask her out sometime."

I couldn't quite imagine it. "Maybe later," I said. "I better do my rounds now." I hurried off before she could propose anything else.

I came in again that night, after two. I bumped into Wayne near Susan's room.

"Awful late," he said, looking at his watch.

"Checking a patient," I said. "He's been trying to die on me for the last couple of days."

He looked at me steadily. "You all right?" he asked.

"Sure."

"You seem distracted lately. Run down."

I looked nervously at Susan's door. "Family things," I said. I'd told him once about the distance between my parents and I.

"Oh," he said, embarrassed. There was an awkward silence for a moment, then he looked toward Susan's room. "Did I tell you we're ending the project?"

"What?"

He turned back to me. "She's fading fast. We won't get anything else. My med student is going to take the computer tomorrow morning."

When he left, I went in and took Susan's hand and sat beside her on the bed, muttered into her ear. The program ran for an hour before she spoke. She said, "Turn around, let me look at you." And she said, "This room, you know, it's so small."

She said, "You know that time I was alone, when I was young? I was lost. I was surrounded by people who towered above me like trees. I kept tugging on sleeves, pulling on arms that felt like bark. You went away. I was looking for you and you weren't there."

"I'm here," I said. I touched her forehead gently, brushed her thin hair from her eyes.

"The ground was so soft. I wanted to sleep, but I knew if I lay down the forest would swallow me — I'd grow into the moss, I'd sprout roots and I'd never come back."

I thought I saw her eyelids flicker a little, but I couldn't be sure.

"All I wanted was to touch someone, to feel skin, to see a face."

I pulled the blanket down a little and opened her gown. Her breasts were veined ivory and I touched them gently. She needed human contact so badly.

When I imagined other women they had always been blurry, passive figures, not quite real. Susan was so real I couldn't contain myself. I kissed her warm lips and moved clumsily over her, trying to be careful, stunned by her beauty.

Early the next morning, Wayne and his student found me asleep in the bed beside her.

She said, "You'll look for me in the forest, but you won't see me. I'll be a sapling in a grove of trees. I'll drink water from the ground." She said it as I sat there and looked at Wayne, at the expression on his face.

He said, "Why?" He said, "Do you know what you've done?" But I didn't try to explain. I knew it would do no good. I knew he wouldn't understand.

I was asked to resign, told to leave the hospital. I wrote letters and made phone calls and couldn't believe I would never see her again. When I learned of her death, months later, I saw the island trees bowing under the invisible hand of the wind and wished it would descend on me until I too was part of the earth.

Out in the middle of the water the wind picks up and pushes the canoe around like a leaf; each stroke is a battle. Every day my shoulders burn and my neck stiffens. I follow a chain of lakes, bumping against inlets and bays until I find the rivers that link them. When I track across the rocking centre of a lake I think of the cold depths, the bass and muskellunge nosing through them, their bodies single flexing muscles with one intent. At my best moments I join them, imagine myself a fish sliding through life, food and motion a thought I repeat with every breath.

At night I sit in front of my small tent and hear her voice whispering through the trees. I stare at the stars splashed carelessly across the sky. Their ancient light pins me to the earth.

The water is deep. I rarely see bottom. Finally, I take my wristwatch off and drop it over the side of the canoe. It falls like a fishing lure, twisting and glinting, diminishing. It winks out and I am free.

The same day, I reach the end of a lake and find the river again. I paddle downstream for hours. It is as if I am descending a flight of stairs. Behind me the land rises; ahead the water becomes rougher and rougher. The river pulls me through itself, a needle on silver thread. Around me its banks rise up like buildings. As I am swept along I see trees climb the rocky walls on twisted feet, half-remembered faces surfacing from the stone. The sun appears and disappears over the edge of the gorge; the water boils around me.

Then the river widens, the water slows and the roar of the rapids fades behind me. Trees crowd in close along the banks and I know I am in the secret heart of the land. I know I have found her at last.

The water beneath me is black and deep. I bend toward it and see my face staring back at me. I cup my hands and drink and drink.

LETTERS TO THE FUTURE

When I talk about small towns, I don't mean those dots on the map that mark a clump of houses, a store or two, a service station. I'm talking about places with history, a courthouse, a school, a decent library, towns that were buzzing with civil industry in the fifties and sixties. True, now they have an uglier face — Taco Bells and car dealerships littering the highway — but each time I'm in a new one I look for the same things: faded civic pride, a collective memory eroded by satellite TV and big box retail, a librarian. It's good to find a librarian who's bored, who's wondering if she's the only one who cares about books, ideas, culture. The only one who thinks high school hockey, drinking in the bush and getting married at eighteen aren't enough.

I read in a magazine once that all happy families are happy in the same way. I believe it's the same with these towns. The good ones are all good in the same way; the bad ones I just try to forget. They're like ghost towns to me, emptied of anything of interest — cars, people, insurance salesmen, motel clerks, birds I've never seen before singing their hearts out in the bushes outside my window.

It goes something like this: I put on my rumpled blue oxford button-down, a pair of faded chinos and a tweedy jacket I picked up at a Sally Ann. I sling a soft nylon bag full of papers, pens and manila envelopes over my shoulder. I go into the library and introduce myself to the librarian. I've thought of calling myself Thornwell Jacobs, but who the hell would buy that? Christ, even in 1936 people must have thought that was an odd name. So it's Jacobs, but I use my real first name, Ted, Theodore if they're old enough to have grandchildren.

The script varies, but the high points are usually the same. This time the librarian was younger than most, but the library had the look they all have: fluorescent lights, institutional carpeting, racks of well-thumbed paperbacks in the popular reading section.

"Good afternoon," I said. My bag thumped on the desk.

She looked up from her computer screen, chewing a lock of her hair, lost in something. "Hold on a second." She tapped a few keys and ran a barcode reader over the book that sat in front of her. "Okay," she said.

"I'm a historian," I said, "here to do some research."

"A historian?" She looked behind her at the stacks of

books for a moment. "This isn't a university," she said. "We don't have an archive or anything like that."

"That's okay. It's newspapers I'm looking for."

By this point they're usually excited — a real live historian rather than some grade nine student, or a retiree working her way through a mystery series.

"There's only one. It isn't exactly the paragon of journalism, unless you're researching the recipe-of-the-week column ..."

"No," I said, smiling encouragingly. "Not exactly. But if you have copies dating back to the forties, I'd be happy."

She looked to the rear of the library. "There's a room full of boxes back there. The *Courier* goes back to the turn of the century, but I don't know how far back our collection goes. They're not very well sorted. We're kind of a small operation here. They should probably be on microfilm, but we just don't have the money."

"That's fine. I'm used to it." In fact, I depend on it. Microfilm's spotty; details, pages, even entire issues, can be lost in the process. The pictures are bad and the text is sometimes impossible to read. Best of all, nobody else bothers to flip through the original musty piles of *Oakville Beavers* and *Saginaw Sentinels*. I wear latex gloves now, though I used to like having black fingertips. I used to get a hard-on when I smelled old newsprint.

"Harriet," she said.

"What?"

"I'm Harriet. If you're digging around back there, you'll be here for a while. You'll need to know my name."

"Of course." I do the Ted thing.

"If you don't mind I'll call you Theodore, too. Ted sounds like someone you'd go hunting with and I don't particularly like hunters."

"You must be popular come deer season."

"I'm a librarian," she said simply, as if that explained everything. She stood up and turned off her monitor. "Come on, then, I'll find you a spot in the back." She came out from behind her desk and started walking toward the back of the library. "So," she said, "what's so interesting about the crappy old *Courier*?"

"I'm looking for stories about time capsules," I said. "I'm writing a book about hope, dreams for the future, what they tell us about the fifties and sixties."

"Really?" she asked, unimpressed. "Haven't we been hearing about their hopes and dreams all our lives? Don't you watch TV?"

I watch the news, the better game shows and history documentaries. Everything else is idiotic.

"Sorry," she said. "I don't mean to give you a hard time, but you know the Boomers recycle the fifties and sixties every chance they get. The Cold War, Sputnik, the Summer of Love. *Leave it to* bloody *Beaver*. What are you going to find that hasn't already had its two hours on the History Channel?"

"You're not like the other librarians," I said.

"It's a long story."

When we reached the back of the stacks she pulled a set of keys from her pocket and opened the door next to the washroom. It was the usual: the employee lunchroom with literacy posters on the walls, a white microwave, a coffee maker, a cylinder of non-dairy creamer. There were stacks of envelopes, paper for the photocopier, boxes of new books. Another door, another key and then a room full of stacked storage boxes on metal shelves.

Harriet gave some strict instructions and then I was alone with piles of newsprint, the familiar smell of it rising from each of the cardboard boxes. People used to think old papers wouldn't last, that their wood pulp fibres would turn into dust after a few years. It fuelled the mad rush to microfilm everything, but they last, all right. I reached into my bag and pulled out a pair of latex gloves.

What I didn't say: I didn't say that every time I stop at a library with its tattered paperback romances, garage sale signs on the bulletin board and lonely librarian, I dream. I dream on a lumpy mattress in my suite at the Red Flag Inn, when I'm driving interstates and Queen's highways. It's a simple dream: all I do is turn a page.

I didn't say: "I said you weren't like other librarians, but I say that to all the librarians. Every town has its own

Harriet and if you drove the roads I've driven you would see yourself at forty, at fifty, at sixty. All these paths leading to the desk and the cardigan and the books and a town lousy with insurance salesmen."

Finally, I didn't say: "I know deep in my bones that it will come to pass that no matter how you feel now, you will marry a hunter, because in the end we are all hunters."

I lay down on my lumpy Red Flag mattress, still smelling newsprint and musty air, and thought about the Crypt of Civilization. Laid to rest in 1940 by Thornwell Jacobs, the father of them all, it sleeps under Oglethorpe University, Atlanta, Georgia. DO NOT DISTURB UNTIL 8113, which is about as far from today as we are from the start of the Egyptian calendar. The man wasn't fooling around.

What will those big-headed creatures of the ninth millennium think of the array of objects stored in the vault? There are six hundred and forty pages of microfilm, a windmill to generate electricity so they can play the phonograph recordings of Hitler, Mussolini and Popeye. There's a quart of beer, for God's sake, a package containing six miniature panties and five miniature shirts, corn plasters and eyebrow brushes, dentures, ladies' stockings, an original script from *Gone with the Wind*, a Donald Duck doll.

In 1996 Sotheby's sold Clark Gable's leather-bound copy of *Gone with the Wind* for two hundred and twenty thousand dollars. A mint quality Donald Duck doll from the thirties doesn't fetch quite the same premium, but it's still worth a few thousand to the right person. *Superman's Christmas Adventure*, a comic book from 1940, goes for four thousand dollars. The market in vintage movie posters is brisk. I could go on and on.

Westinghouse may have coined the phrase "time capsule," for the 1939 World's Fair, but it was Jacobs who started it all with his 1936 article in *Scientific American* and the building of the Crypt. Jacobs really thought someone would wait until 8113 before cracking that seal, that crowbars and shovels would fall out of fashion. He forgot that most of the tombs in the Valley of the Kings have been empty for a thousand years.

The fourth morning a bird I'd never heard before sang from the bush outside my window. It had a long, liquid call that rose and fell and rose again. It was the sort of sound that might tug at someone's heartstrings in a country music song or paperback romance. I peeked out the window, half expecting to see Harriet out there singing away. It was a blue bird, with a long thin tail. I threw half a bagel at it from the bag on my bedside table and it gathered up its feathers like the skirts of a matronly woman and took its music elsewhere. Down at the Red Flag breakfast nook I had cereal and toast, avoiding the $6.95 breakfast buffet of congealed eggs and fossilized bacon.

I had only made it through two boxes the day before. Fifty papers a year times twenty years equals one thousand closely printed issues. That's a lot of stories about weather and school board meetings and car accidents. I had become tired of the back room and started taking my papers to the stuffed chairs in the front and reading them there. I could see Harriet from the chairs, behind her counter. She didn't laugh much, but she didn't seem particularly sad either. She had that look people have when they're listening for a footstep in the hallway, a knock on the door.

You'd think that after doing this as long as I have that I wouldn't be distracted by librarians, or by the papers themselves, that I'd fire through them like a speed reader, but it's a long and boring slog, so the interesting things stick in my mind. For instance, in three days of reading I discovered that until the end of the war there was a POW camp just outside of town. In a forties' issue I found a picture of a funeral service being held there, the casket flag-draped, iron cross prominent as German officers in greatcoats stood around with flowers in their hands.

Nobody remembers these things: the scandal involving the mayor in 1949, hints of sexual impropriety between the lines; the polio scare one summer that kept kids from local pools; civil defence meetings; the return of Korean War vets; a woman named Julia Casket who lived to be ninety-eight; a carpenter who installed peepholes in every house he worked on for fifteen years; the grade school that was built on a decommissioned army base, unexploded munitions heaved up by frost in the playground. These towns hardly deserve their pasts. The paperback romances must seem more real.

I was in the archive room reading about a series of mysterious sheep deaths in 1955 when Harriet knocked on the open door behind me and poked her head in.

"It's tuna salad today."

We ate our lunches together now. I had brought my own on the first day, but I'll admit it was a rather half-hearted attempt — a chocolate bar and a doughnut. She'd looked at it and said, "You can't be serious." Instead, she gave me half her roasted pepper, Asiago and pesto sandwich, laughing at my expression when I bit into it. She had a nice laugh, a slightly crooked smile, slightly crooked teeth.

"I'll bring you a whole one tomorrow," she said. "I can't watch you eat that crap."

Today was tuna salad on thick multigrain, flecked with tomato, celery and green onion, layered with crisp romaine. "You've really got a way with sandwiches," I said.

"I'm sure you say that to all the librarians."

"You don't really seem ..."

"Like a librarian? You mean, what's a girl like me doing in a place like this?"

"I wasn't going to say *that*," I said.

"Close, though," she said. "Here's the condensed version. My mother was the librarian for years; I worked here through high school. Then I was off to university and halfway through my master's degree when she got sick. I came home to take care of her. I took on her work at the library because nobody else wanted to do it. The ladies who do the mystery book club and the high school girls who stack the shelves part-time certainly weren't interested. So I was here and didn't feel like going anywhere else. I'm still here."

I felt nervous for a moment. I touched the piece of paper folded in the front pocket of my chinos. "Maybe you can help me," I said. "I've found something."

"Better than the POW camp? Better than Julia Casket, unmarried until the age of ninety-six?"

"I've been bothering you," I said.

"You're kidding," she said. "What do you think I do all day once the books have been shelved and the ladies have their Agatha Christies?"

"I've found the story I was looking for."

"Oh. Congratulations." She took a bite of her sandwich. "So you're leaving, then?"

A poster on the wall that read HOOKED ON READING showed a trout with a fishing rod pulling a book out of a pond. It seemed to have captured her attention.

"I want to finish going through the rest of the papers to see if there are others. Then ..."

She tilted her head quizzically, reminding me of the bluebird.

"There's a time capsule I'd like to find," I finally said. "I'd like to dig it up."

"Can you do that?"

"There are thousands of time capsules buried around the world; most of them have been forgotten. If nobody digs them up, nobody will know what the people who buried it wanted to say. We're the people they wanted to find this stuff, after all."

"So you just start digging holes?"

"That's the problem. People misplace them. Sometimes they're in building cornerstones, sometimes long paved over, sometimes forgotten entirely."

"I'm not much good with a shovel," she said.

I pulled a photocopy of the story from my pocket, unfolded it. "There's another way you can help."

The picture was of a group of people standing in a field. In front of them was a sealed time capsule the size of a child's casket. Low-slung buildings skulked in the background. There were shovels in evidence (always a good sign) and surveyor's stakes. The headline read: TIME CAPSULE TO BE BURIED AT NEW SCHOOL. Students and staff had written letters to the future, local businesses were involved.

Harriet squinted at the picture. "That silver thing is the time capsule, isn't it?"

I nodded. "They were going to call them time *bombs*."

She looked closer, her nose nearly touching the paper, staring at the halftone dots of the photograph.

"Half the school burned down when I was a kid. We were all pretty happy about it."

"It's still there, though?"

"They rebuilt it. It looks like they're standing on the playing field in the back." She looked thoughtful. "Did you like high school?"

"Sure."

"It's the interesting people who have the worst time of it in high school, the people who can't be the same as everyone else. Don't you think?"

"High school was fine," I said. "High school was a breeze."

I changed the subject, asked her about surveyor's plans, architect's drawings.

"The town hall should have them. They'll make copies for a small fee, but it might take a day or two."

"It's been waiting fifty years," I said. "I can wait a couple of days."

She knocked on my door at the Red Flag that night. The news was on.

"I know the clerk," she said after I let her in. "He told me your room number. I hope you don't mind."

"No," I said. I was suddenly aware of my toe sticking through the cheap cotton of my right sock, the small pile of dirty clothes by the bed.

"I thought maybe you'd be sick of the food here. You might want a real dinner."

Her house was small, on a well-treed lot. Buttery yellow light spilled across the lawn and the bushes in the front yard. She pulled her pickup into the driveway, gravel crunching under the tires. "I'm not really the truck type," she said as we got out. "My car's in the shop. This is my dad's."

Her father was retired, basketball player tall, had to bend slightly as he went through doorways. When he sat on the couch, his knees were almost level with his head. I took the easy chair across from him and we both glanced at the pictures on the walls and the faded wallpaper as if they were deeply intriguing. Harriet was making cooking noises in the kitchen. Finally he said, "Historian."

I waited a moment, but that seemed to be all he was going to say. "Yes," I replied.

A minute passed. There was a small pile of dust beside the fireplace that someone had forgotten to sweep into the pan. "You fish?"

When I was a child there were days on the water with my father and his friends. I remembered the metallic sound of the bass they hadn't bothered to kill thrashing against the aluminium hull of the boat, the men pissing off the side as their empties piled up by the Styrofoam cooler.

"No," I said.

"You should fish. We've good fishing here."

There was a picture on the mantel of Harriet as a teenager. You could see the woman she was now latent in her younger face, though her hair was shorter, her cheeks rounder. For a moment I wished I had known her then, could have taken her out in my rusty Ford Escort. We would have driven with the headlights off down the rural routes past rustling fields of summer corn. Things would have been different.

We marinated in awkward silence and what felt like silent disapproval. Harriet came in to save me.

"Dad," she said. "For God's sake get him a beer." She winked at me. "The poor man's obviously dying of thirst."

Harriet drove me back to the Red Flag after dinner and coffee and after her father had livened up enough to tell a few stories about his days with the Parks Service. There had been glances between us during dinner; she had shown me family photos. We sat there in the truck in the parking lot for a few minutes, a not uncomfortable silence between us. *I should write this one off*, I thought. *I should pack my bags tonight and pay my bill in the morning and drive to the next town.*

Instead, I turned and looked at her upturned face, the slightly crooked shadow of a smile. "Um," I said. "Do you want to come in?"

She nodded and I must have looked surprised, because she laughed. "Come here," she said and grabbed my ears. She tasted of coffee and burnt sugar, her skin faintly of popcorn.

We lay there on the lumpy bed in my room after the kissing and all the rest of it. I had filled the plastic ice bucket from the machine down the hall and she held a chip of it under her index finger and ran it down my chest in a cool line. I left my hand on the curve of her hip.

"I've been thinking about Julia Casket," she said, "who married at ninety-six for the first time. What does that say to you?"

"What should it say?"

"Maybe it's never too late."

"To get married?"

"For anything," she said. "To change your life."

I thought about the other librarians I had known, the long ribbon of road that stretched behind and ahead of me. It was hard to imagine doing anything else.

"I think Julia wasn't like the rest of us," I said. "I think Julia is the exception."

She propped herself up on her elbows and looked at me. "You're the historian. You've been reading all about people's dreams. Didn't you ever look anyone up and see how they turned out?"

"No," I said. "I never looked anyone up. But I think we're probably all disappointed in the end."

She sat up, pulling the sheet around her. She suddenly looked vulnerable; it tugged at something in me. "I'm just saying that," I said.

"It's getting late," she said. "I better get home."

I stood in the doorway in boxers and a T-shirt as she drove out of the motel courtyard in her father's truck. She'd looked at me from the parking lot and said something I couldn't hear. I waved, anyway.

"I've got a shovel and a spade," I said. "I'll use the spade to cut the turf, the shovel to dig out the earth."

"You sound like my father," Harriet said. She stood holding a flashlight, the beam pointed at my feet. We were behind the school, just beyond the edge of the playing field. Surveyor's flags bloomed from the grass, marking the squeals of my metal detector.

"Well, maybe it doesn't really matter what I use. I just haven't had an audience before."

"So you never ask permission to dig up someone's lawn?"

She had suggested we talk to the school board, or at least the caretaker, maybe even have a reporter there. "Most of the time I strike out. It's better to appear with a time capsule in hand than with a shovel and a half-baked idea."

I dug and Harriet held the flashlight beam on the ground and I started to hope we wouldn't find anything. Two hours later the ground was pocked with small craters. I'd found an old beer can, unidentified rusty chunks of metal and a handful of nails. Cinders a bit below the grass gleamed darkly, remnants of the fire. I stood there for a moment, leaning on the shovel, feeling the sweat trickle down my side. Harriet scrutinized the site plans, the light from her flashlight yellowing as the batteries faded. "I was sure this was the spot in the photo," she said.

"We've still got two markers left." But I could feel the empty ground below us, the secrets it would not give up. I would dig twice more, come up with a handful of nails, then I could just drive away without looking back. I could start again somewhere else, anonymous again.

At the next flag the capsule announced itself with a hollow clank. My shovel blade hit it, about half a metre down. I stood there for a moment, the shovel still deep in the earth.

"Bingo," Harriet said. "Jackpot."

It looked like an ancient artillery shell, the metal marked with soil, stains and a long scratch from my shovel. It took the two of us to lever it out of the hole.

"I feel like a grave robber," Harriet said. We were both dirty, sweating, perched by the unearthed capsule and the hole it had left behind.

"More like an archaeologist," I said.

"They're not really that different, are they?" She rubbed her hands together, working a cramp out of her fingers. The flashlight faded and winked out, leaving us in the dim light of the half-moon and stars.

"So we fill in the hole and then what? Some sort of celebration?"

"I'm usually by myself," I said.

"We should celebrate," she said. "Doesn't your room at the Red Flag have a tub?"

Her face was turned toward me, a pale smudge in the night. I was unsteady. It felt like the sea was about to sweep my little boat out from under me.

Back at the Red Flag we splashed around in the narrow tub, my legs tight around her hips. I soaped her back. A cold beer wept condensation on the toilet seat by the tub. The remains of a pizza littered the countertop; green pepper and olive debris spilled from the box. I rubbed shampoo from the tiny bottle into her hair. The things we do when we're trying hard not to think.

Well-scrubbed, we tumbled around on the sheets for a while. It was better than the first time. Half-asleep afterward I felt her pull her arm out from under me, a kiss on the temple light as the footsteps of a mosquito. "I have to leave again," she said.

"Run, run, run," I mumbled as she dressed.

I dreamed about coffins and dead people. I woke in the small hours and searched around the room, feeling hollow as a straw, before I remembered we'd dropped the capsule off at the library after we'd filled in the holes. It was safe, tucked away in the back room.

There was no birdsong in the morning. Its blue source had left for parts unknown. Consequently, I slept late, missed the breakfast buffet, the insurance salesmen who had checked out en masse that day, the opening of the library. When I finally arrived, a knot of people were gathered at the time capsule — *my* time capsule.

Harriet approached, eyes bright. "People love it," she said. "I cleaned it up this morning, put out the word."

They were running their grubby hands over its surface, chattering excitedly.

"Here," Harriet said. "I want you to meet someone."

"It could have been damaged," I said. "You should have talked to me first."

"I thought you'd be happy."

"Oh, I'm happy," I said. "I'm over the moon."

She gave me a strange look and then tapped the shoulder of a woman standing near the capsule, interrupting an animated conversation. "Mona," Harriet said. "This is Theodore, the historian I told you about."

Mona beamed at me, her grey hair in tight curls around her head. She clapped me on the shoulder. "Great going, Indiana Jones." She motioned to the capsule. "I'm in there, you know. My grade seven class wrote letters to the future and sealed them inside. I'd completely forgotten until Harriet told me this morning." She touched the top of it lightly. "You wouldn't believe the memories …"

"That's fantastic," I said. "Really." I smiled tightly at the two of them. "I'll just be a second."

I went to the back of the library, opened the door with one of the keys I'd copied from Harriet's set one day while she was out and went into the storeroom. There were two unread boxes of *Couriers*. I sat on my chair and started sorting through them. I'm supposed to be discreet; I'm supposed to keep my distance. It was remarkable how much I'd screwed up.

It took twenty minutes before Harriet came back. "People want to talk to you," she said.

"So I gather."

"The mayor wants to do a whole opening thing tomorrow night for the six o'clock news. The TV and everything. They want you and me to say something."

"Did I ever tell you about the blue bird?" I asked her.

"What?"

"Every morning it sits outside my window at the Red Flag and sings. The first time it's okay, the second time, too, but not day after day. Who can take that? The same sad little song day after day after day."

She didn't look very happy, but I hadn't asked her to go to all this trouble. I hadn't said a thing about it. "What's really going on?" she asked.

"How is *this* research? This dog and pony show, these people running their hands over an *historical artifact*? What do they know about history?"

"It's theirs, isn't it, the people of this town?"

"They don't deserve it."

"Jesus, Theodore. It *is* theirs." She spoke slowly, as if she were piecing something together. "This is their town, their time capsule, their mayor. They buried it and they're the ones who are supposed to open it. You'll still get to look through the contents."

The capsule was slip, slip, slipping away. "You're right," I said, conciliatory. "I get carried away sometimes. It's hard for me, when I've spent so much time looking. I've been disappointed before."

"You had me worried," she said. She smiled. "So you'll talk to the TV people, tell everyone about your research?"

"I'll put on a show," I said. "Don't worry, I've done this before."

What makes one person able to do something others can't? Julia Casket getting married at ninety-six, for example, or a bank robber sticking up the local credit union. It's a matter of will, being able to cross the line. The difference between a bank robber and yourself is not the gun, the note, the ski mask — these are props. The difference is that standing there in the line-up for the teller the bank robber has the will to pull out that gun and make his demand.

That evening after Harriet went home I drove over to the library and parked by the dumpster in the back. I put on my carpenter's belt, clanking with tools, and opened the back door with one of my copied keys. The time capsule sat on the table mid-room, gleaming in the light of my flashlight. I had a closer look at it. The case was in two halves, held together by a line of bolts. Fifty years underground had left the bolts pitted and scarred, though the whole thing had survived remarkably well. I treated each bolt with penetrating oil and pulled up a chair while I waited for it to work.

I once found an x-ray of a child's foot. A holy relic from back in the days when they x-rayed everything, when the shoe store in the city had a fluoroscope and you could wiggle your toes around and see the bones move. The bones were striated, ghostly, flesh just a shadow on the film. Something about it made it hard for me to throw away, though it wasn't worth anything.

The bolts came off. Wrench, hacksaw, small drifts of metal filings piling up on the table. More than enough evidence to convict, certainly. But who really cares about a time capsule?

I pried the top cover open like a coffin; for a moment I envisioned a skeleton, hands folded across its chest, a toothy grin. But the light of my flashlight found only a scattered mess of paper, some boxes. I smelled the scent of the past released.

Sometimes I pick through looking for choice morsels and leave the rest for whomever might find it interesting. This time I took it all. Paper, disintegrating plastic dolls, cardboard tubes and boxes. I left the plaque TO BE OPENED OCTOBER 12, 2052, inscribed in tarnished silver with the names of important people. Idiots put the date on the inside, not the outside.

Back at the Red Flag I spread the contents on the bed. One box held children's letters. I tossed it aside. One had letters from the old mayor, town council, various important, and probably dead, people, also worthless. Next some newspaper photos, including the one with everyone standing by the time capsule. Then there were samples from various merchants: squares of cloth, beauty supplies, a glass bottle of Coke, dolls from the toy store, tacky to the touch. They were just dolls — no Minnie Mouse, no Donald Duck. There were also magazines, a book with a garish dust jacket, some movie posters.

In the end I set aside five comic books in brown paper, a package of baseball cards, a Roy Rogers and Dale Evans lunchbox and thermos and three movie posters in cardboard tubes. It was a good find, not the best I'd had, but good.

I packed my clothes and the collectibles in the car, settled my bill with the night manager. I felt clumsy putting my bags into the car, like I didn't quite fit into my skin. Then I realized I could take the leftovers and put them back into the capsule, seal it up again, stay for the opening, make up some stuff for the TV people. It wouldn't be hard.

I took the back way to the library, car tires crunching up the lane, headlights off. It took three trips to move the leftovers into the building. I left them by the capsule and went to dig through the trunk for my tools.

When I came back in, the pile had been moved and there was a pool of light at one of the reading tables. I stood holding my flashlight and tools, the door clicking shut behind me.

She didn't look up. She sat at the table holding a piece of paper.

"I'm bringing them back," I said. My voice sounded too loud. Harriet didn't look at me. I went over to the capsule and put down the tool belt.

Then she looked up. "Whatever you took isn't worth what you think it is."

I started to say, "I didn't — " and then I thought better of it.

"I know you're dropping these off, that they're worth nothing to you."

I didn't say anything. She didn't sound angry. I couldn't tell what she sounded like.

She was still looking at the piece of paper. "I was excited. I couldn't sleep. I wanted to come out and look at it. So, naturally, I was surprised to find it open and empty. I went to find you, to tell you. Then I saw you loading your car at the Red Flag." She looked up. "So what did you get?"

"Some comics," I said finally. "A lunchbox. Stuff like that. Collectibles."

"And you've done this before? You're not really a historian?"

I nodded.

The letter in her hand shook a little. "It's funny," she said, "what has value and what doesn't. Those things you took are meaningless, pop culture crap. But the letters, the photographs, these pieces of people's lives. Nobody wants to pay for these."

"I'll return the other stuff," I said.

She shook her head. "No, you take it. Like I said, it's not worth anything to us." She held up the letter. "This is

Mona's letter, written when she was twelve. Her whole life waiting to happen. Have you ever read any of these letters? Or do you just throw them away?"

I started to answer, but she interrupted me. "No," she said, "I don't want to know. I don't want to hear anything else you have to say. Go find another town. Go find another librarian."

If I had said anything before taking my tools and getting into my car and driving away, I would have told her I *had* read the letters. I would have told her that they're all pretty much the same, that I doubt Mona would have said anything different from any other twelve year old. *I was here. Remember me.* Some crap about world peace, that the people of the future will be wiser and kinder. All the things we never are and never will be no matter how long we wait to open the time capsule.

It wasn't the last time I saw her. A year later I was up at the university, deep into the library stacks, when I heard a voice I recognized. I looked around the corner and saw her sitting at one of the study tables with some students. They were laughing and there was a boy who couldn't have been more than twenty-five or so next to her, his arm casually around her shoulders. He obviously thought he was pretty smart.

I could have gone up to her, said hello, as if we were old friends. I could have asked if she was finishing her master's degree. I could have told her that she had been wrong, that the things from the time capsule really *were* worth something, that collectors paid nearly a thousand dollars for them. I thought about it, but my meter was running out and I had to go.

SAFE

That summer the big news was the trial of a washed-up film star who had cooked and eaten his agent and a producer, serving portions of them to guests at a barbecue on his deck overlooking Malibu Beach. His defence was summed up in a single phrase: "Revenge is a dish best eaten outside." It provided some variety for people sick of stories about two-headed cows, fish with legs, the image of Christ Our Saviour in the pattern of burns on a young girl's back. Sales of the star's barbecue sauce jumped several hundred percent.

Marilyn found herself following the trial with a queasy fascination. At Kensington Market, beside signs that read GUARANTEED SAFE, tabloid headlines screamed the details in thirty-point bold. She leafed through them as the Chinese woman at her regular stall wrapped her vegetables in layers of plastic to protect them from the dust. Marilyn never *bought* the papers; they were just junk food for the soul, an antidote to the meat and potatoes of her discontent.

The summer had been dry, hot and brittle; forest fires had crept southward, grown large and ravenous from the lack of firefighters. The resulting sunsets were wonderful, but they came with a fine dusting of soot and ash that blew across the city and lodged in every crack. She and Derek often watched the evening sky from their balcony after dinner. He would sit quietly in his chair, the light painting his sallow skin with the illusion of health.

"There is a bitterness that lies at the heart of beauty," he said once, referring to the sunset. He'd been reading philosophy for months. She had hoped it would give him some perspective, turn his thoughts away from himself. If anything, it had made him more cynical.

Often at night Derek would cough both of them awake. He would get up and pace the dark rooms of the apartment, his feet padding across the wooden floor they'd refinished when they first moved in. Sometimes he'd speak softly and she couldn't make out the words. She would curl up in the middle of the bed like a knot in the twisted sheets, a castaway. Outside, as dawn approached, the birds sang as if the world had never changed.

She taught English three days a week to the immigrants who still came to the city. There were rumours that the government encouraged them, told the police to ignore them when they moved into abandoned houses. Nobody wanted to admit that a third of the city's population had left since the disaster.

She stood in front of fifteen or twenty men and women in a classroom without air conditioning, feeling the sweat on her forehead, the small of her back. "Apple," she said holding one up. "Is this a safe apple?" The voice of the class was an echo of her own. "Doctor," they said. "What's the diagnosis?"

The actor's bizarre crime inspired copycats. A butcher in Pittsburgh was found to be selling pies made from ground dog and cat and the remains of vagrants who'd "vanished" in his neighbourhood. People brought their pets inside. An office worker in Boston poisoned his boss, was arrested driving the body home in rush-hour traffic. Marilyn's fingers grew dark with tabloid ink.

In early August her class graduated, giving her three weeks off before she took on another. She held a small party for her students in the school lounge. They listened to one of her jazz CDs and ate noodles, hot dogs and spring rolls. She accepted their gift: a small silver clock. She knew it was contraband, the fruits of someone's salvage operation; they couldn't have afforded it otherwise. It was really quite lovely, but just touching it made her cringe. After they left, she guiltily dropped the clock in the dumpster behind the school.

She cycled to the market and bought the makings of dinner, splurging on Swiss chocolate and oranges. Ahead of her, a young family, all wearing surgical masks, crossed the street pushing a wheelbarrow full of used VCRs.

Dust still filtered down upon the city; there had been little rain to flush it from the air. When she got home she found the elevator was broken again and she had to walk four storeys. Inside the radio was on, chattering to the empty living room. She put her groceries away and then walked to the balcony where Derek lay in his chair, a damp towel over his face.

"Why don't we take a trip?" she asked. "Let's get out of here."

"Where would we go?"

"Anywhere," she said. "Into the country. To the coast. Australia."

"Right," he said. "We'll just stock a ship with provisions and set sail for the colonies."

The greyish towel erased his features. Marilyn looked at him, the blue veins under his skin. There was a small dressing on his left arm. "You were at the hospital."

"Just a check-up," he said. He peeled the towel back like the lid of a canned ham and his face appeared, squinting at the light. For a moment he was a pale, fractious child. A year before, his hair had come out in clumps and, though it had grown back later, it still looked somehow unfinished, like a poorly made wig. She suppressed an impulse to smooth it down.

"What did they say?" she asked.

"There are six-year-olds with leukemia in beds in the

halls because there isn't any space in the wards. They've got people staying in an old motel by the lake. That's what they said."

"Who was it this time? Richardson?"

"Richards. Dr. Richards. No, she's not working with me any more. This one told me not to come in unless something dramatic happens. I think they're getting sick of me."

"'Dramatic'," she repeated. What was dramatic was the small stroke he'd had four months ago. He'd woken up confused and slurring his speech. He had a hard time controlling his right arm. His right eye wouldn't open properly. Her heart, which she thought was shrunken and dry, leaped and fluttered in her chest, an injured bird.

"A small incident," Dr. Richards had said. The hospital had been crowded; the staff looked as if they hadn't been sleeping well. Everybody knew the health care system was in trouble. She expected to go to the hospital with Derek one day and find it closed, out of business like half the stores in the city. "Just a little stroke," Dr. Richards had said. She held up Derek's CT scan and pointed to a small dark area.

A stain, Marilyn thought. *A stain on the brain*. Was she being irrational? The doctor gave Derek anticoagulants, which made him light-headed and caused nosebleeds but seemed to help. She wanted to ask why they didn't know what was *really* wrong with him, but she knew she'd get nowhere. He wasn't the only one like this.

"Why don't we just leave?" she asked. From the street she heard an argument in a foreign language, a faint siren rising and falling.

"Can you see me on the deck of a cruise ship?" he said. "Not that we have any money."

"No," she said. "For good, I mean. The hospital's not doing anything for you anymore."

"You know we can't," he said. He frowned slightly. "It's not possible."

"I'll find another job," she said, knowing it was useless. She used to dream of a small place in the country with climbing roses, nesting birds in the eaves. Somewhere safe. But the realm of the possible had diminished for them in the last few years, as it had for most people. She had once imagined the future as an open field, something she could explore at her leisure. Now it was just a procession of small, dim rooms she was forever being herded through.

"Just watch the news," he said. "It's the thirties out there. Soup kitchens and hobos. The cardboard jungle."

"I know what it's like."

"Then you know you're dreaming." He got up unsteadily and walked slowly toward her. "Look," he said. "I'll make dinner tonight. My treat." He brushed her cheek with his dry lips as he shuffled past her into the apartment. She stood on the balcony, the sound of clattering pots behind her. A thin, dark line of smoke drifted over the horizon. This was what her soul would look like, if she'd believed she had one: tenuous, drawn-out, holding its shape out of habit and stubbornness.

After dinner she announced she was going out. Derek looked at her as she picked up her keys and played with them absent-mindedly. He was settled on the couch in front of the TV, waiting for a nature documentary or a game show. He liked the one that awarded a couple a large sum of money, provided they spent it according to an arbitrary and peculiar set of rules — they had two hours, but could only buy blue things, or they had to shop with blindfolds on, that kind of thing. She knew the documentaries reminded him of his days as a biologist. She supposed the game shows were just another form of escape.

"I'm visiting Rosa," she said. He looked slightly hurt. "Oh, for God's sake," she said. "It's not like I have any other friends."

"It's not our fault they moved."

"They've not all gone — we just don't see them anymore." She occasionally ran into old acquaintances on the street, or at the museum when she took her classes on field trips. They had survivor conversations: where to buy cheap food, good clothes; gossip about those who had moved away. They didn't really *talk*; people kept their problems to themselves these days, their heads down.

"I'll give her your regards," she said as she closed the door.

Rosa lived in an old house near Eglinton, one that had been abandoned by its original owners. She had opened it up, cleaned it out and bribed or sweet-talked various city departments into giving her power and water. Marilyn could hardly imagine it. She hadn't even tried to sneak into bars when she'd been underage.

They sat in the living room and sipped red wine, which was said to ward off radiation. "You look tired," Rosa said.

"Doesn't everyone?"

"Not me," she said. "I'm on holiday now."

Rosa also taught at the English school. She claimed she could always identify former pupils by the way her Jamaican accent had mingled with their own. "I have another visitor coming," she said. "An old friend of ours."

"Who?"

"You'll see," she said. "He'll be here soon. You'll be pleasantly surprised."

Samuel arrived not long afterward.

"Most grateful," he said, accepting a glass of wine. He was tall and thin and spoke like the professor he had once been, his voice smooth as water. Two years earlier he had worked at the English school with them. He had conducted his classes as if they were university courses, the ones he could no longer teach. He gave off an air of genteel disgrace. Marilyn had heard the rumours — plagiarism, some sort of sexual scandal — but neither had been confirmed. It hadn't stopped her from flirting with him and, one night, after a staff party and a few drinks, she had almost taken things too far. He'd left the school at the end of that term and she had felt relieved, unsure what might have happened if he had stayed.

"Samuel lives in the disaster area now," Rosa said.

Marilyn was startled. "It was evacuated," she said. "Sealed off, wasn't it?"

"More or less," Samuel said. "People can come and go if they're not too obvious about it."

"You're not alone?"

"No, no," he said. "You'd be surprised how many people live there. It's a far simpler world."

She looked at the soil caked on his hiking boots and imagined the radiation streaming invisibly from them.

"I know what you think," he said. "But we're healthy. I haven't been sick for a long time. Everything grows there, the birds sing, there are deer in the fields. It's not as bad as they say."

While Rosa was in the bathroom Samuel looked intently at Marilyn and smiled. "Rosa says you want to leave the city. You're not happy. Why don't you come for a visit — see for yourself?"

"Wrong direction," she said. "I want to get *away*."

"Pity." He gently took her wrist.

"There's still a pulse," she said. His fingers were warm and smooth.

"Just barely," he said. "Just barely."

Back at the apartment, Derek was half-asleep on the couch. "They lost their hundred thousand," he said. "Underwater shopping. And there was something about polar bears and pollution, the dirtiness of the world."

"As if *that's* news," she said. She helped him up from the couch. "It's nice to come home to a report."

He went into the bathroom. "That's not irony, is it?" he called out behind him. "Because it sure sounds like irony."

She toppled onto the bed and lay there, smelling the familiar sheets, the his and hers of them mingled together. She caught herself wondering if there was any soap left in the little nook by the washer and dryer, then thought, *Is this what we've been reduced to, matters of laundry?*

When he came out she rolled onto her side and he lay down next to her. She put her hands on his chest and felt his ribs shifting as he breathed, moved her hands farther down to the love handles that even his illness hadn't removed completely. She slid her hands lower, desire suddenly warming her like a sip of brandy.

He shifted uncomfortably as she stroked him. "Sorry," he said. "It's this medication."

It had been a long time. "Right," she said. "The medication."

"I can help you get there," he said.

"Don't bother." She got up from the bed and went into the bathroom. Through the door she heard him sigh loudly. She turned the tap on, filling the room with the sound of water.

She had a hard time sleeping, though Derek had dropped off quickly. In a few hours he'd probably be coughing, then wandering the apartment, half-awake and muttering. She remembered Samuel's hand on her wrist, the intensity of his gaze. She imagined the disaster area slowly becoming overgrown, animals and a few people living quiet lives there as the buildings and roads crumbled away to nothing.

Rosa called a day later. "Samuel's taking a crew from the BBC into the area tomorrow afternoon," she said. "There's space for you if you want to go along."

"Why would I want to go along?"

"It's just a day trip," Rosa said. "He asked me to ask you. He said you'd find it interesting."

Derek was in the second bedroom, the one they'd converted into an office. Every so often he managed to get a few days of long-distance consulting, usually through old colleagues. This time it was on a wetlands study in the north. She knew he'd be on their ancient computer for hours, chatting with the scientists involved in the project, telling them how much he wished he was still in the field. His excitement made her strangely sad; for the first time she'd wondered if they gave him these small tasks out of pity.

"I'd go," Rosa said, "but there's only room for one and he wants it to be you."

"I'll think about it," she said.

Derek spent the rest of the day in the office. She could hear him talking to the other project members, offering suggestions, trying to make the experience last as long as possible. She felt, but restrained, a strong urge to leave, to walk through the overgrown grounds of the university or the busy stalls of Chinatown. It was as if staying now would somehow compensate for the trip she would take later. She called Rosa that evening.

"A trip with Rosa," she told Derek the next morning. "To see her aunt in St. Catharines."

The film crew had rented a ridiculously large off-road vehicle; it looked vaguely military and menacing, all hard angles and welded steel bars. She sat beside Samuel in the back, listening to his tour guide patter as they drove eastward on highway 401. His leg rested warmly against hers.

"The population gets older as we get closer to the area," he said. One of the crew held a small tape recorder toward him, while another filmed the housing developments beside the highway. "The older people aren't as worried about the possible danger here; they're more rooted."

Samuel directed them northward, toward farmland and patches of forest. At the perimeter, there were large, faded warning signs: the symbol for radiation like the propeller of an airplane. They stopped so the crew could set up their camera and film the truck driving around the barricades. Marilyn and Samuel sat on the grass at the side of the small country road, just inside the perimeter.

They could have been on a picnic. It was warm and slightly breezy, birds and insects drifted over the road, ignoring the border. "It doesn't feel any different," she said. The film crew had put on white plastic jumpsuits and dosimeter badges when they stopped.

"It's an arbitrary line," he said. "Just like a national

border. Who's to say this piece of land is any different from that one?"

She looked at the film crew. One of them was holding a Geiger counter in the air while the cameraman filmed him. "People like them, I suppose."

They drove through abandoned towns, past signs promising exotic jungle cats, country markets, McDonald's. It was comforting to be a passenger. She felt strangely passive, caught up in something much bigger than herself. Occasionally there were signs of habitation: cows in a field, mournfully chewing the long grass; a car moving down a dusty road; recently cut trees. From a hilltop they saw the small shape of the power plant down by the lake, transmission lines stretching out from it uselessly, a squat spider snared in its own web. Even through the telephoto lens of one of the crew's cameras, it looked intact, as if it had never spilled its poison over the land.

It was late afternoon when they pulled up at the Victorian farmhouse where Samuel lived. The film crew dropped off some of their equipment and then vanished for a few hours of shooting before the light died. She and Samuel walked around the property, Samuel pointing out the large vegetable garden, chickens squabbling in a coop behind the house. "It's lovely," she said.

He nodded. "Whoever owned it was kind enough to leave it fully stocked when they left. It was simple to get things running again."

"Maybe they thought they'd be coming back."

"I doubt it," he said. "People were afraid of the area right from the beginning. They have no idea what it's really like."

When the film crew returned, it was dark. "We'd like to stay the night," Liam, the producer said to her. "We've more footage to shoot tomorrow."

She looked at Samuel — his face was neutral. "Fine," she said. "I'm sure I can find a spare bed."

At dinner the crew looked alarmed when Samuel set out a meal of chicken, corn and potatoes. "No offence," Liam said. "But we've brought our own."

Samuel shook his head. "There's no need to be afraid," he said.

"Sorry," Liam said. The crew took sandwiches and drinks from a cooler. "You're welcome to join us though."

Samuel glanced at Marilyn. She looked at the food on her plate and knew it was a test. When she finally took a bite of chicken, she realized she didn't know if she'd passed or failed.

Samuel knocked on her door late that night. He entered quietly and sat on the edge of her bed. "What do you think of the place?" he asked. He was a dark shape in the dim starlight that came through the window. His hip rested gently against her leg.

"Why are you living here?" she asked. "Why not somewhere else?"

"You live out there," he said. "You can see what a mess it is — everything's falling apart. Here we're safe from all that; we're free. The radiation doesn't matter. The radiation's meaningless. Living here is like being born again."

"You're not afraid?"

"No," he said. "I'm not afraid. Not at all." She felt his hand on her hair and shivered a little. "And you don't have to be either. Why don't you stay?"

The feeling that had come over her in the truck still held her. It was as if simply being in the disaster area had taken away her will. This poison was nowhere and everywhere, was invisible. It would be so easy to just embrace it and abandon the fear that haunted her.

She reached up and touched his face, tracing it with her fingertips. She could feel her heart racing. "Come here," she said. She pulled him closer and he lay down beside her.

"Will you stay?" His hand brushed her breasts.

"Don't talk," she said. She rolled over and covered his mouth with hers. His fingers burrowed through the blankets until they found her bare skin. She closed her eyes.

After he left, she lay there watching the stars slowly wheel past the window. Orion appeared, as it did over their balcony when she and Derek sat out at night, drinking Irish whisky and listening to jazz. Things *looked* no different from here, but it was obvious that this was a different land. Lines had been crossed.

In the morning she walked into a scene. "Careful," Liam said. They were filming two of the crew members playing badminton on the lawn of Samuel's house. Everyone was wearing their white radiation suits. It seemed appropriately surreal.

"Sorry," she said.

Liam motioned to the camera operator to take a break and then looked at her.

"Let me show you something." He was carrying his Geiger counter. He held up the small device. "Three hundred and forty microrads," he said. "More than twenty times the acceptable level. Everywhere we travelled yesterday it was above a hundred." He motioned her over to the chicken coop. "Have a look," he said. He pointed to a small bundle of feathers on the dusty ground inside the coop.

"What am I supposed to see?"

He turned the bundle gently with his gloved hand and she saw it was a chick with two heads. It tried feebly to raise them. "The future," he said. "That's what you're seeing. I don't know what's going on between you and your friend, but you should try and make him understand: this isn't a healthy place to live."

He went back to his camera, leaving her at the coop. She stared down at the struggling chick, unable to look away.

She was still there when Samuel came up behind her. "It's a beautiful morning," he said.

"Have you seen this?" She pointed at the chick.

He reached over the fence and picked it up. He didn't

seem surprised. "It happens," he said. "It's not important." With a quick twist of his hand he wrung the chick's neck.

She shuddered. "How can't it be important?"

He looked at the tiny body in his hand. "We're not chickens, are we?"

She thought of Derek wandering the apartment alone last night, how she'd felt when he'd had his stroke. She was possessed with an almost unbearable sadness. "I'm not going to do it," she said.

"Do what?"

"Stay here. It's not real. It's not *my* world."

He looked at her intently. "You're serious. Even after what happened between us?"

She thought about the night before, how she'd closed her eyes. He could have been anyone. "I'm sorry," she said. "Your freedom costs too much."

As the truck approached the city, they saw thunderclouds gathering on the horizon. On the radio the news was live from the Los Angeles courtroom — the film star's trial was at an end. The documentary crew listened intently as the announcer reported a hung jury, a mistrial.

"Bloody Yanks," Liam said. "Typical."

She realized she didn't care any longer. Guilty, innocent, it didn't seem to matter.

After they dropped her off, she walked the four storeys up to the apartment. The air was sour and muggy in the stairwell. Inside, the TV played a documentary on whales to an empty room. For a moment she imagined Derek had left, had another stroke, been taken away. He could be cold and still in an overcrowded hospital somewhere. But he was on the balcony, his pills and a glass of orange juice on the table.

She stood by the door watching him. In a moment, she would slide it open and go out. They would never *really* be safe, she realized, but maybe that wasn't the only thing that mattered.

SARAJEVO

They were driving over to his mother's when he felt it. He wasn't sure what it was at first. When he realized he was nervous he nearly laughed. He could have been back in high school, driving his father's car to some freckled girl's house for a first date.

Julia looked over at him. "What?"

"Nothing," he replied, glancing at her. "Bad drivers."

She smiled and returned to her reading, her hair falling over her eyes.

It was snowing quite heavily as he took the exit to his mother's place. The car skidded a little on the ramp and he felt a second's panic, the wheel loose beneath his hands. "You could slow down a bit," Julia said absently, not lifting her head from the magazine.

He felt a sudden desire to let go and see where inertia and ice would take them — just close his eyes and slide through the barrier, the grass, the housing developments, let the car fold around them like origami.

The wheels caught on pavement and they continued under the bridge and past gas stations and decorated houses to the townhouses near the lake.

When they went inside he give his mother a quick hug and headed past the rest of the family in the living room to the toilet. He could hear them all through the door as he sat there — adults talking, kids yelling, excited about the presents stacked under the tree.

His mother hadn't fixed up the bathroom when she moved in. Her passion for redecoration had died with his father: nobody now to appreciate her talent for paint and ornament, no one to grumble about the cost. She had only added her towels and toiletries, her collection of porcelain mice.

Eventually there was a tap on the door. It was Julia. "Are you alive in there, Peter?"

"Save me a spot on the couch," he answered. "I'll be out soon."

When he finished he took a long drink, splashed his face and swallowed a couple of Aspirin from the cabinet. He didn't really want to leave. It was comforting being alone among the rose petals and disinfectant, the glowing row of small bulbs along the top of the mirror.

In the living room Peter sat beside Julia and sipped a beer. His mother looked at him quizzically and he knew she wanted to ask him about it. Dan, his brother-in-law, finally blurted it out.

"So what's it like over there?" he asked. "What's it really like? Quite the shit hole, eh?" Peter's sister, Jane, looked at him quickly, angry at him for swearing in front of the boys.

Sure enough Steven started singing, "Shitty, shitty, shitty."

"Dan, really," Jane said and then turned to Steven, "Quiet honey, Peter's talking."

He shrugged. "You've seen the news. It's like that."

"We've read your pieces in the paper — they're very good." His mother bustled around with a bottle of wine. "I just haven't had time to keep up with everything else. You know how busy things get."

"So, they shot at you?" Dan again, swirling his beer.

"No, not really," he said. "Usually I drive around and bribe people to tell me stories. It's pretty dull."

Dan frowned slightly, ready to ask another question, when little John tripped over an electric cord and started howling. He ran to Jane for consolation and Peter relaxed, knowing he was off the hook for the moment.

His mother had been taking cooking classes at the local community college. "I even brined the turkey," she announced proudly as she laid it on the table. She set out platters of mushrooms and wild rice, sweet potatoes with pecans, green beans with almond slivers. He looked at the little piles on his plate and noticed their colours matched the curtains and the upholstery. He moved them around with his fork for a while and then attacked his wine, drinking a glass quickly, refilling it from the bottle in front of him. He listened to the conversation, sipping steadily.

Jane talked about putting John in daycare. "We're starting next month," she said.

"Aren't you worried?" his mother asked. "There are some shifty operators out there, you know. They're keeping kids in dirty basements, feeding them macaroni every day. It was on the news."

Jane grimaced. "If I don't get back to work soon I'll go crazy. He'll be fine."

He caught the tail end of one of Dan's stories. "... found them screwing on her desk, right there in the office. If she's not fired she'll be transferred for sure."

Julia shook her head at this, distaste on her face.

After dinner, the kids wandered off to play and they opened a bottle of port and sliced some cheese. Dan took a swallow of his drink and shook a cracker at him. "Come on, Pete," he said. "You've got to have some stories to tell. Stuff that didn't make the paper." Every time he talked to his sister, Peter expected to hear Dan had run off with his secretary or embezzled funds from his accounting firm. He looked as if it could be coded in his genes, like heart disease, or a propensity for hair loss.

He was right, though. There *were* stories that had never

been printed. Peter's editor had been pressing for more human interest material: the last theatre group in the city; how to avoid sniper fire; how to collect food and water. "People are sick of hearing about massacres," he'd said. "Find some new angles. We need more features people won't skip over on the way to the comics. STRING QUARTET IN THE RUBBLE, BULLET-PROOF PIZZA PARLOUR, that sort of thing."

"All right," he said to Dan. "I had dinner in a bomb shelter last week."

Everyone was quiet. He could feel their eyes on him, their interest, their need to confirm the blessedness of their own lives.

"The town I was in was being shelled, so I hid in a basement with a woman and her family.

"Every so often a shell would land nearby and the place would shake. We thought, *This is it, the house is going to collapse*. This went on for hours, so the kids got hungry, and we decided to have a meal. There wasn't much in the root cellar except onions, beets and potatoes. She had bread and I had chocolate and a flask of brandy.

"It was wonderful. As good as this meal in its own way. There were thuds above us every so often, but we managed to ignore them enough to talk. The woman had been to school in Paris, so she and I talked in French. Her husband had been taken away the month before. She hoped he had been taken to one of the concentration camps, but feared the worst.

"She said that the men who took him away wanted to rape her and her daughters, but the leader of the group had been the daughters' school teacher and he stopped them. I asked her why she stayed and she said, 'Where would I go? Paris? This is my home. I'll never leave it.'"

Peter took a sip of his port, a bite of cheese. He felt Julia's hand searching for his on the couch. He allowed her to rub his fingers.

"What happened?" Dan asked.

"They stopped shelling that night. They took over the town and herded all the Muslims into one of the enclaves. I left and went back to the city."

"Poor woman," Julia said. "What happened to her?"

He shrugged. "She could be anywhere."

There was a respectful pause before the subject changed to something more comfortable.

They left early. He told his mother he was tired, a little under the weather with the jet lag, an oncoming cold. When he walked outside into the winter night he felt something shift inside him. The streetlights were orange-yellow, the sky glowed from the reflected light of the city. He imagined lying in his mother's front yard, letting the flakes sift over him until he was hidden under the drifts. Julia's face was pale in the faint light, watching him.

She drove and they were quiet for most of the trip back into the city. The lights of the suburbs retreated. Cars passed by with their cargos of parents and children returning from other Christmas dinners. The clockwork world ticked on.

They woke up late to sunshine, the city brilliant with snow. He went out for the paper and some croissants, stepping carefully over the drifts. Cars frosted like dough-nuts lined the street. Plows scraped the roads clear. The air was crisp, the sky pale blue and flawless. He felt like an astronaut walking gingerly across the surface of a new planet. He hardly knew how he got there.

"Let's talk about February," Julia said at breakfast. She spooned sugar into her coffee. "There's so much to do when you get back." She wiggled her eyebrows at him. "My parents are going to drop all sorts of hints this after-noon, you know. They want to know when you're going to make an honest woman of me."

"I'm not sure I'm up to it," he said.

"What?"

"Your parents. Going out today."

"My parents," she said, "are mad for Boxing Day. *And* they didn't see us yesterday."

"I still feel under the weather," he said. "Maybe I'm coming down with something."

She felt his forehead. "No fever."

"Nevertheless, I feel like hell."

"I can't go alone," she said.

"Sure you can. What did you do before you met me?"

"That's not the point." She frowned at him the way his mother used to, when he was growing up.

He took four Aspirin, washing them down with orange juice, and then dabbed his forehead with a damp cloth.

"Fine, then," she said. "I'll go. I'm sorry you'll miss it."

"Send them my apologies," he said. "Sorry." He went back to bed.

After she changed and left, he wandered around the apartment in his boxer shorts and T-shirt. He turned on the TV, but all that was on were old sitcoms and holiday specials he couldn't bear to watch. He sat on the sofa Julia had brought with her from her apartment when she moved in and picked at its fraying fabric. He thought about the night before, the lie he had told and what it all meant. He remembered the face of the woman he'd stayed with, the faces of her daughters, her mother toothless and wrapped in a black shawl.

He went out in search of a movie at the video store and was mildly surprised to find it closed. He'd almost forgotten it was a holiday. He bought a couple of magazines from the 7-Eleven instead. One of them showed the upcoming year's styles: young men and women in ill-fitting, garishly coloured outfits. They had the same slightly hollow-eyed stare and rough attire of the people he'd seen crammed into sputtering old cars or walking with suitcases along the side of the road. Displacement and war as a fashion statement.

He was curled under a blanket on the couch when Julia came home. The TV was trying to sell something. He felt her hand on his forehead and opened his eyes. "I'm awake," he said.

There was melting snow in her hair and on her overcoat. Outside, the cold muzzle of darkness pressed against the glass of the living room window. "You missed a nice evening," she said. "My mother gave me some soup to bring home for you. She's very concerned."

"Soup for the sick," he said.

"Or something."

"You don't believe I'm ill," he said.

She looked at him seriously. "You don't look like it."

He waved the remote at the TV until it turned off. "Do you know I lied about that story last night?"

"It didn't happen?"

"I changed the ending," he said. "I made everything turn out all right, but it didn't. The militia came in the morning and hauled everyone outside. I recognized the commander — I'd interviewed him the previous week. We'd played cards together. He wanted to know if the story on him was finished, that I'd sent it to the paper.

"He made me come back to the command post with him and play gin rummy and drink plum brandy. Then he brought me back to show me what they'd done.

"They had killed the woman I had dinner with. She was lying in the street with her neighbours. Her daughters had been sent off on buses. All the Muslim boys from the town had had their throats cut and their cocks put in their mouths."

He was quiet for a moment. His own voice sounded strange to him, the way it sounded when he transcribed his interview tapes.

Julia sat quietly with her eyes closed. He couldn't read

her face. Then she stood up and started clearing his dinner dishes from the coffee table. "I don't understand," she said.

"What?"

"Why you're still doing it. Why you want to see these terrible things."

"It's my job," he said.

"And dinner last night. You lied to everyone. You lied to *me*. Did you think *I* needed to be protected, too?"

"It's not entertainment," he said. "It's not dinner chatter." He picked up the blanket and folded it over the back of the couch and then walked into the bathroom to brush his teeth.

She came to the doorway and leaned against the frame. "It's not good for your gums to do it so hard."

He shrugged, spat and rinsed. "It wasn't easy," he said. "I came back to holiday dinners and Dan's stupid jokes. People I used to know are dead."

"I'm sorry about that," she said. "but I don't want you to be next. I watch the news every night and I have a hard time sleeping. I keep thinking I'll hear your name on some report. I have bad dreams ... and now this. You can't keep doing it."

He reached out and touched her shoulder. "I'll be back," he said. "I'll be careful."

In bed she radiated worry. He tried a few exploratory caresses, but she turned away. "Another time," she said in a small voice. After she fell asleep he lay in bed listening to the muted traffic sounds from the street below, her quiet breathing.

He thought about the morning when the militia had hauled him and the family in the basement onto the street. He had been half-asleep, lulled into the illusion of safety by the end of the shelling.

He had not recognized the commander, a drunken, brutal-looking man. He heard cries from down the street, gun-shots. He looked at the men in front of him with their battered rifles and grim faces and knew he was very close to death. He pleaded with them. He threw out names of other commanders he'd interviewed, waved his press cre-dentials, his passport. He didn't look at the woman or her family.

Finally they took him aside and the commander told him he would give him something to write about. He made sure Peter had the spelling of his name right before he had his men kill them. He smiled. He said, "Put this in your notebook: the commander smiled as he ordered the executions and the journalist pissed his pants."

He woke up early, light just beginning to stain the sky. Julia was sleeping quietly. He walked into the living room and stood by the window, cold seeping through the glass.

He could leave. He could pack quietly, slip out of the apartment and be on a plane before she woke up. He took a step back from the window, breathed slowly and the impulse passed. Eventually, he returned to bed.

When it came time for him to leave, it gave him no relief to see Julia wave for the last time as he walked through the departures door at the airport. He thought escaping her worry and questions would lift something dark and heavy from him, but it did not.

He changed planes in Amsterdam and called her while he waited for his connection.

"How was your flight?" she asked.

"Fine," he said.

"Did they give you a good meal?"

"Sure," he said. "The usual."

"When are you coming back, Peter?"

"I don't know," he said.

He listened to the faint sound of her breathing. A baggage cart rumbled past. A loudspeaker muttered something. The silence stretched on and on.

ACKNOWLEDGEMENTS

Previous versions of the following stories have been published as follows: "Outside" in *Chatelaine*, "Sarajevo" in *Grain*, "Ring Around the Moon" as "Shadow of the Moon" in *Event*, "The Land His Mother" as "The Southern Cross" in *Fiddlehead*, "Nasty Weather" in *Event*, "Heart of the Land," in *Prairie Fire* and *The Journey Prize Anthology* 12 and "Small Accidents" as "Deer" in *Fiddlehead*.

This book would not have been possible without the support and guidance of many people: my family — Alan, Jeanette, Aileen and Alison — who served as my sounding board and my first editors; Mike Chaffe, Deanne Telford, Vicki Black and Rick Maddocks, who lent insight to works-in-progress; Linda Svendsen and George McWhirter at UBC's Creative Writing Program and the members of the graduate fiction workshop there; my agent Carolyn Swayze, who found it a home; and Joy Gugeler, who helped make it better.

OTHER RAINCOAST FICTION

Tracing Iris by Genni Gunn
1-55192-486-2 $21.95 CDN $15.95 US

Sounding the Blood by Amanda Hale
1-55192-484-6 $21.95 CDN $15.95 US

Quicksilver by Nadine McInnis
1-55192-482-X $19.95 CDN $14.95 US

Write Turns: New Directions in Canadian Fiction
1-55192-402-1 $24.95 CDN $19.95 US

Slow Lightning by Mark Frutkin
1-55192-406-4 $21.95 CDN $16.95 US

After Battersea Park by Jonathan Bennett
1-55192-408-0 $21.95 CDN $16.95 US

Kingdom of Monkeys by Adam Lewis Schroeder
1-55192-404-8 $19.95 CDN 14.95 US

Finnie Walsh by Steven Galloway
1-55192-372-6 $21.95 CDN $16.95 US

Hotel Paradiso by Gregor Robinson
1-55192-358-0 $21.95 CDN $16.95 US

Rhymes with Useless by Terence Young
1-55192-354-8 $18.95 CDN $14.95 US

Song of Ascent by Gabriella Goliger
1-55192-374-2 $18.95 CDN $14.95 US